Quinn was frowning, shaking her head. "I just don't know if I can—"

He cut across her, relieved. "See, Edward. She can't do it anyway—"

"She isn't saying she can't do it. *She* was going to say that doing it inside six months is going to be a stretch."

He felt a flamethrower blasting his ears. Putting him in his place, which, even looking through his jaundiced lens, he could see he totally deserved. He inclined his head by way of apology, which she accepted with her eyes.

He forced out a smile, opening his hands to seem reasonable and calm, which he wasn't. "I'm just saying that if you were to turn the project down on the basis of being too busy, then—"

"It won't make a blind bit of difference." Edward's voice was sharp as glass. "For the third time, William, the terms of the will are this: you inherit Anthony's estate only when the Lisbon Hotel has been up and running for three months; you must take personal charge of the project from here on in; and Quinn is to be your interior designer. It isn't negotiable."

Dear Reader,

Welcome to my Lisbon story! I was lucky enough to visit this gorgeous city last year and was struck by how many once beautiful but now sadly neglected buildings there are—a consequence of complicated inheritance laws apparently! Of course, I immediately began to think about how I could create a story centered around one such building.

After a few false starts (it happens!), I devised an inheritance story of my own, wherein my tortured hotelier hero, Will, and kindhearted interior designer heroine, Quinn, are forced to take on the renovation of a dilapidated Lisbon building and launch it as a hotel. Not such a hardship, surely, considering all that warm Lisbon sunshine, fabulous seafood and those delectable Portuguese custard tarts! Sadly, since Will and Quinn aren't exactly the best of friends, they don't see it that way. But soon, as the old animosities start to collide with an undeniable, growing mutual attraction, they find they've got more to wrangle with than rotten floorboards and cracked pantiles...

I hope you enjoy reading Will and Quinn's journey to their happy-ever-after as much as I enjoyed creating it.

Love,

Ella x

BOUND BY THEIR LISBON LEGACY

ELLA HAYES

Recycling programs for this product may not exist in your area.

ISBN-13: 978-1-335-59677-2

Bound by Their Lisbon Legacy

For questions and comments about the quality of this book, please contact us at CustomerService@Harlequin.com.

TM and ® are trademarks of Harlequin Enterprises ULC.

Harlequin Enterprises ULC
22 Adelaide St. West, 41st Floor
Toronto, Ontario M5H 4E3, Canada
www.Harlequin.com

Printed in U.S.A.

After ten years as a television camerawoman, **Ella Hayes** started her own photography business so that she could work around the demands of her young family. As an award-winning wedding photographer, she's documented hundreds of love stories in beautiful locations, both at home and abroad. She lives in central Scotland with her husband and two grown-up sons. She loves reading, traveling with her camera, running and great coffee.

Books by Ella Hayes

Harlequin Romance

Her Brooding Scottish Heir
Italian Summer with the Single Dad
Unlocking the Tycoon's Heart
Tycoon's Unexpected Caribbean Fling
The Single Dad's Christmas Proposal
Their Surprise Safari Reunion
Barcelona Fling with a Secret Prince
One Night on the French Riviera

Visit the Author Profile page at Harlequin.com.

This one goes out to my sons, James and Matthew, who will probably never read it but will hopefully get to Lisbon one day and enjoy it as much as I did!

Praise for
Ella Hayes

"Ella Hayes has surpassed herself with this delightfully warm romance. It keeps a reader on their toes with its twists and turns. The characters are believable and you can actually visualize the scenes through the exquisite descriptions. This book ambushes your senses and takes the reader on a beautiful journey with heart-stopping moments. A wonderful relaxing read."

—*Goodreads* on *Italian Summer with the Single Dad*

CHAPTER ONE

WHAT THE HELL was Edward saying to Will? Because Will was exploding off his chair, gesticulating at the solicitor so hard Quinn could practically feel the waves of his fury pulsing through the soundproof glass. And then his head whipped round, his eyes seeking hers, locking on.

She felt her blood draining. Why was he looking…no, glaring at her like this? She was only in line for some small token of Anthony's affection: a keepsake or maybe a donation for the homeless shelter where she volunteered. That was why she'd been asked to come, to be 'on hand' at the reading of Anthony's will. That was why she was waiting out here while he was in there for the important business.

Outside the family. Outside the boardroom. Waiting for a small bequest. Made sense. Nothing else did. Could! Because Anthony had more than done his legal duty by her already. Giving her a home when Dad died. Caring for her, supporting and guiding her, even granting her the interiors contract for the Thacker Hub hotel in Kensington when she was just starting up her business, still wet behind the ears. She owed Anthony Thacker big time, and he owed her precisely nothing. But now Will was bruising her with his eyes, and he wouldn't be doing that without a reason, would he? Not when, for years, he'd barely looked at her at all.

She cut free, forcing her gaze to the floor. What was going on? She didn't know Will, had never quite got the chance to get to know him, but it didn't take a microscope to see he was bleeding hard, wounded by whatever Anthony had put in that will.

But why would Anthony do that—hurt his son—when he'd loved him so fiercely, respected him for the great job he was doing as Thacker's Head of Business Development? Anthony had admired Will's drive, his sharp intellect. Not so much his gambling and his casual sexual encounters, admittedly. They'd used to fight about that apparently, but the fight was because of the love, because Anthony wanted better for Will.

That was how she'd read it anyway, from the distance of her own life, and it tallied with all the things Anthony had said during those long chemo afternoons: that he loved Will more than life itself, wished he'd handled things better, drawn him in closer, especially after his mother left, drawn him in and held him there instead of losing his grip, messing up…

Confessional talk. Out of character for Anthony. She'd said to him that it was Will he should be talking to, that it wasn't too late, but he'd said it was, that Will would see it as a selfish act, just a father trying to salve his own conscience before the inevitable happened. She hadn't known what to say then because what did she know about the way Will saw anything?

That was the thing about Will. Everything about him was a guess. Like guessing he'd gone from being shyly kind to her when she'd first moved in, to being distant, because she'd been grieving too hard for Dad at the time, feeling too displaced in the strange house to respond to him properly. And like guessing that the reason he didn't hang around for long during his uni holidays was because he really did have better places to be than the Cotswolds house, better things to do than joining her and Anthony for pub lunches and mad rural hikes.

And of course, Christmas at home couldn't possibly compete with skiing in Chamonix, staying at his friend Jordan's family ski lodge, could it? Easter? Guess he did the right thing there, never coming home at all, staying 'up' so he could revise, because it paid off. He got a First, not that she went to the graduation. There were only tickets for family. Nothing she didn't know, but when Will said it to her, it had felt like a stone sinking in her chest.

That was the stone she could feel again now, sinking lower. And it was so stupid, so wrong for them to be distant like this when they had Anthony in common, this terrible grief to share. And no, Anthony wasn't *her* father, and no, he hadn't been the easiest person, but was it any wonder after losing his eldest son to a speeding white van like that, then losing his wife eighteen months later to some hedge fund manager with a place in Jersey, all while steering Thacker Hotels to ever greater success? He wasn't perfect. He'd made mistakes, especially with Will, but he'd been good to her, and she loved him, missed him, wanted to talk about him. But Liam the Scumbag had gone, found some other girl to love, so she couldn't talk to him, and Sadie was a diamond, always a good listener, but she hadn't known Anthony, whereas Will…

Her heart twisted. Talking to him made sense. And she'd thought he'd see that, want to talk to her too, but when she'd touched his arm at the funeral, trying to build a bridge, all she'd got back was the same curt nod he used to give her when he arrived at the hospice—dismissive. *Hurtful!* And then he'd stepped back, turned a cold shoulder.

And she didn't deserve that, didn't get it, because Will wasn't heartless. If he was, he would never have hovered in her bedroom doorway all those years ago with his kind blue eyes and his hands pushing into the pockets of his jeans, saying he was sorry about her dad dying, that he knew how she was feeling, that if she wanted to talk—

'Quinn?'

Edward... Standing in the open doorway, holding the door she hadn't heard opening. Could he see her mouth going dry, her blood trying to march backwards? If so, it wasn't showing on his face, and it certainly wasn't changing anything because he was opening the door wider, stepping aside for her.

'Could you come in now, please?'

Quinn was shaking her head, frowning. 'I don't know if I can—'

He cut in, relieved. 'See, Edward. She can't do it anyway—'

'No, Will!' Cutting right back in, pinning him hard with her clear gold-brown gaze. '*She* isn't saying she can't do it. *She* was going to say that doing it inside six months is going to be a stretch.'

He felt a flame thrower blasting his ears. Putting him in his place, and rightly so. He'd been rude, letting the old wounds bleed too freely. He inclined his head by way of apology, which she accepted with her eyes.

Her eyebrows drew in again. 'The problem is I have other work scheduled, other commitments…'

'Which *I* understand…' He forced out a smile, opening his hands to seem reasonable and calm, which he wasn't. But he'd thrown his toys out of the pram with Edward once already and that hadn't got him anywhere, so calm and reasonable was the only option. In any case, whatever he thought about Quinn Radley, this one wasn't on her; this was on Dad, one hundred fricking percent. He gave a little shrug. 'I'm just saying that if you were to turn the project down on the basis of being too busy then—'

'It won't make a blind bit of difference.' Edward's voice was sharp as glass. 'For the third time, William, the terms of the will are this: you inherit Anthony's estate *only* when the Lisbon hotel has been up and running for three months; you must take personal charge of the project from here on in and Quinn is to be your interior designer. It is not negotiable since Quinn's personal bequest is contingent on her doing the work…' His gaze shifted to Quinn 'Work which you were already discussing with Anthony, I believe?'

She gave a strange sideways nod. 'We talked about it…' And then she was closing her eyes, evidently reining in some emotion. 'When Anthony first bought it, I mean, before he was diagnosed…'

In other words, before the project rolled into the long grass. Why couldn't it have died there instead of coming back to bite him? Blasted hotel! He'd *told* Dad it was going to be a massive waste of time and money.

Granted, Bairro Alto was a prime location, but the building was sprouting grass for goodness' sake! Roof, walls—every nook and cranny. As for the interior, that was a whole other can of festering worms. And all for what? A paltry eighteen en suite bedrooms and one master suite! Payback period—for ever! Dad's insane passion project, a little *amuse bouche* because he loved Lisbon and 'fancied a challenge'. Maybe it didn't say much for his sense of filial duty, but he'd intended to slap it back on the market the second it fell into his hands. So much for that plan!

'I understand, Quinn…' Edward was shuffling his papers together. 'You weren't expecting a rush job. If you're tied to other clients for the time being, then we must wait.'

Except it wasn't *we*, was it? It was *he*, Will, who must wait for Quinn, work with her. *Her* of all people, at Dad's behest!

He felt his blood rising, a vice tightening somewhere. Had Dad not had eyes to see with?

Had he *not* noticed him opting out of family life circa six months after Quinn arrived? Had he never asked himself why?

He ground his jaw. Of course not, because he wasn't Pete. Pete, he'd have noticed. Every blink, every breath! But he'd never been captain of the rugby team, had he? Holding up the trophy, muddy and triumphant. He'd never had swimming medals to line up on a bedroom shelf. No bear hugs and back slaps for Will. Just the searing devastation of losing his brother, best friend. The light in the room; the light in the dark. All the dazzling light.

God, how he had missed him. The thump of his schoolbag going down on the hall floor; the rhythm his feet made walking; the different, leaping rhythm they made when he was bounding up the stairs. The sound of his voice, that rich chuckling sound of his laughter, that bright flash of his smile. He'd been everything. To him. To Dad. To Mum…

How he'd had to fight to fill a single toe of Pete's shoes. To be seen. Noticed. Taking Mum cups of tea that she'd let go cold. Pulling the blanket up around her shoulders when it slipped. Rubbing her feet to win a pale smile. Pushing himself at school to make them both sit up. Top grades across the board—better than Pete ever got.

Not enough to stop Mum taking up with Gabe

the hedge fund jerk though, was it? Not enough to stop her from leaving, making the hole he was trying to fill even bigger, but he'd banked the hurt and pushed on harder, faster, focusing on Dad. Duke of Edinburgh Gold! Maths prize! Science prize! Inching his way into Dad's field of view. Working admin jobs at Thacker HQ in the school holidays to impress him, riding shotgun in the BMW like Pete used to. Weekends, he'd pitch in, working on the old convertible with Dad to please him, because that car was Dad's pride and joy.

Jeez! He'd been smashing it six ways to Sunday, feeling pretty good about himself, so close to worthy that when Quinn first came, hollow-eyed and beautiful, aching with grief over her dad, he'd thought nothing of reaching out to her, wanting to be kind, because why wouldn't he want to soothe her when he *knew* her pain, could feel it living inside him every single day that Pete wasn't around. But she'd curled like a leaf, shutting him out, which he got too, because pain could be like that, wanting to keep you all to itself. He'd thought time would do its healing work. And he was going to uni, anyway, spreading his wings…

Oh, but he hadn't bargained on coming home to find that Quinn was the new apple of Dad's eye. Quinn this. Quinn that. Cooking together, laughing at their little in-jokes. He'd told himself it would be petulant to react, that Dad and Quinn were bound to fall into a rhythm since they were living in the same house. He'd reined in the negativity, tried not to mind, but then came that Christmas pub quiz, Dad's friend coming in, wanting to join their team, Dad saying he could if Will didn't mind moving to another team because of the numbers—*Will*, not Quinn by the way—saying it in such a way that he would have looked like an utter stick-in-the-mud if he hadn't smiled and got up. Enough to turn a stomach, hollow it out. Heart too. That night he'd decided. No more fighting for his place. Easier to back off, leave them to it.

But now he couldn't back off, make himself scarce. Heaping insult onto injury, not only had Dad saddled him with this hare-brained, budget-busting renovation project from hell, but he'd saddled him with the cuckoo in the nest as well—the cuckoo he'd spent the last decade trying to avoid! And all he wanted—*all* he wanted—was to move quickly, get the infernal thing done so he could get his life back, not to mention his inheritance. But now Quinn wasn't even sure she could fit him in!

He inhaled to cool his blood, slid his gaze through the window to the sea of high-rise buildings bleeding shadows in the low February sun.

There had to be a workaround. Some way of speeding things up. Roof, façade, walls, windows. Three floors, eighteen beds, bar, dining, reception. His stomach pulsed. *Maybe...*

He turned to look at her. 'Could you work piecemeal?'

'Piecemeal?'

She was looking at him as if the concept was alien. Well, he could relate! Everything about this was alien, the opposite of comfortable.

He licked his lips. 'Look, I'm no expert on old buildings but I imagine renovation isn't a linear process. Some areas are going to be ready for your input ahead of others. I'm just wondering if you could dovetail into the workflow so we can keep everything moving.'

She see-sawed her head, weighing it up. 'It's a possibility. The challenge would be keeping the finished areas clean.'

'Would that be especially hard? I mean, have you seen the building?'

'No. Only photos. And some preliminary sketches from the architect.'

'Same here...'

Which suddenly seemed ludicrous, given what lay ahead. He felt a tingle, resistance trying to bite, but he tamped it down. No way round it. This was a needs-must situation.

He drew in a breath. 'Quinn, do you think you could make time for a quick site visit?'

She blinked. 'Go to Lisbon, you mean?'

Too tempting not to deadpan.

'Ideally, yes, given that that's where the building is.'

Her eyes held him, busy replaying the last three seconds, and then suddenly her face split and she was chuckling, giving herself up to laughter, a sound he could feel somehow in his own body, feel tugging a smile up through him, and he didn't want to give in to it because Quinn was the one making it happen, pitching him back to the Cotswolds house—her and Dad, shoulder to shoulder at the kitchen table, laughing over some stupid video on her phone—but he couldn't hold back the rumble in his chest, couldn't keep his traitorous cheeks from creasing. At least he wasn't alone. Edward's lips were twitching too.

And then she was coming back down to land, rolling her eyes at herself, touching two fingers to her sweet, curving lips, catching one short, clean fingernail with her teeth. 'In case you're worried, I'm not usually this dumb.'

'I'm not worried.' Not about her anyway. He pulled himself straight. 'So, about Lisbon; if I can fix up a visit with the architect, could you spare a day?'

She lowered her hand. 'I could, depending on the day, obviously.'

'Would a weekend be easier?' Anything to speed things up. 'Assuming the architect could make it…' And assuming she didn't mind leaving her boyfriend behind. If she had one. He let his eyes run loose. Eyes, lips, dark corkscrew curls grazing the smooth curve of her cheek. Of course she had one! She'd been lovely at seventeen, and she was even lovelier now. Excluding himself, what man on earth could walk past her?

Her mouth twisted to the side. 'A weekend *could* work…'

Do the decent thing, Will.

'If it helps, you could bring your other half, on the company, obviously, make a weekend of it.'

Her gaze flickered for an intriguing beat, then sharpened. 'Thanks for your consideration, and for the generous offer, but that's not the issue…'

And none of his business either, if her tone was anything to go by. But then, suddenly, she was sighing, frowning, shaking her head a little.

'I'm sorry. That didn't come out quite right.' She inhaled and then her gaze cleared. 'I don't have another half, but even if I did, I wouldn't let him get in the way of work.'

Why was he getting an *ever again* vibe? Was it her mouth? That little bit of tightness there. Or her eyes? That touch of bruised steel.

She gave a little shrug. 'The reason I'm havering is because I volunteer at a homeless shelter. I have my regular nights, but sometimes things can change, so I'd need to check the schedule before committing to a date.' Her lips set. 'I don't want to let them down.'

Surprising about the boyfriend, but this wasn't. He didn't know her ins and outs, which was the way he liked it—why he'd always changed the subject quickly if Dad struck up about her—but no denying she was the warm, caring type. Hands-on.

Sitting with Dad through all his chemo sessions. And when Dad moved to the hospice she was invariably there when he arrived—running late because of work—taking up the slack—*his* slack—which felt like a slap. Doing so easily, smilingly, all the things he had to grit his teeth to do. Raising Dad up, the skin and bones of him, to help him drink. Blotting his mouth afterwards. Taking his hand. All the touchy-feely stuff that should have come naturally but didn't. But it did to Quinn. Warmth was her superpower. And at the funeral she'd aimed it right at him, put her hand on his arm…

He pushed the thought away. 'Kudos on the shelter work.'

She blushed. 'It's nothing.'

He felt his brow pleating, a weight shifting

inside. It was categorically not nothing. How he spent his downtime was nothing. No doubt Dad had moaned her ears off about it, painting him black. Gambler! Womaniser! So what if it wasn't quite like that. So what if he'd let Dad think it was for the craic. It still amounted to nothing. Was that what she was thinking now: that he could do better with his time? It wasn't in her gaze, but who knew?

He looked at Edward. 'Do you happen to know anything about Dad's architect?'

'Yes.' Edward consulted a note. 'She's called Julia Levette. She's English, living in Lisbon, has a lot of experience with old buildings and the pertinent regulations. I've got a number here.'

'Great.' He switched his attention back to Quinn. 'I'll give Julia a call; see if she can offer us some possible dates.'

'Good.' She nodded a smile then turned to Edward, making to move. 'Are we done now?'

'No…' Edward's lips pursed. 'Not quite.'

She sank back, and he felt his heart sinking too, beating fast irregular beats as it went. The solicitor was drawing two envelopes out from underneath his papers. And then his eyes flicked up, moving between them as he talked.

'As I explained to you both earlier, Anthony adjusted his will to incorporate the stipulation about the Lisbon property just a month before he passed. At the same time, he gave me these envelopes: one for you, Quinn, and one for you, Will.' He slid them over. 'I don't know what's in them, just that Anthony wanted you to have them today.'

High white laid, Dad's stationery of choice. His name writ large, that resolute line scored underneath. *Blue-black ink.*

He felt his throat tightening, a vague burning sensation building behind his lids. Dad had used the fountain pen, the one he'd gone halves on with Pete to buy him a million Christmases ago, the one they'd taken ages over choosing so it would be exactly right.

He closed his eyes. Of all the stupid things to stir him up.

CHAPTER TWO

Dearest Quinn,

I write this wondering if I'm doing the right thing, so be assured, if you conclude with your smart head and warm heart that I'm not, then don't think any more about it. Live free and be happy, because I don't mean for you to carry the burden of my mistakes.

But, selfishly perhaps, and especially now that you know the contents of my will, I need to air them, put them into context, tell you things I haven't spoken about before. If I fall short, forgive me. When it comes to matters of a personal nature, I don't communicate well.

You'll recall me telling you about my boarding school days, where survival depended on not showing what was going on inside. Sadly, it's been a hard habit to break! But I must try now so you understand my anguish over Will, my desperate need to make amends for not being the father he deserved.

How to begin? With Pete, I suppose, the son I could never talk about. You must have found it frustrating, but there are things, guilts I cannot reveal, even in a letter—even to you, who always listens so well. For now, suffice it to say that Pete was a lively boy. Charismatic. Sporty. Pete made it easy for me to seem like a good affectionate father, because he won trophies, medals, tangibles I could applaud openly.

Will was—is—so very different. Thoughtful, reserved, sensitive. As a boy he looked up to Pete, adored him, lived a little in his slipstream, like younger brothers do. But Pete adored Will equally, looked after him. I see so clearly now that Pete got me and Judy off the parental hook by assuming the role of Will's caretaker, freeing us to pursue our own lives and careers.

Truth to tell, Quinn, Pete was the glue in our family, the paper that covered our cracks. When he died, those cracks all gradually reappeared—in mine and Judy's marriage, in the entire fabric of our lives.

But here's the thing: after the initial devastation of Pete's death and those first few terrible weeks, Will mustered a strength I never knew he had. I won't go into everything here because to think of it breaks my heart. Let's just say that I think, in his own way, he was trying to fill the void his brother left, trying to make good.

Sadly, as you know, Judy went on to meet someone, too sick of me and my faults to try any longer. She thought that since Will was doing so well at school he should stay there, keep living with me—thought that the combination of Jersey and getting to know her new partner would be too much upheaval for him after everything he'd been through already.

Another painful time, but Will rallied again, asked if he could work for Thacker in his school holidays. And he started helping me with the Morgan, which wasn't fully restored back then, getting to grips with the engine far better than I ever did.

Don't get me wrong, we were still feeling Pete's loss, Judy's absence, but Will seemed to settle. Sometimes he even seemed happy. You probably don't remember seeing him like that because you'd just come to us, full of sadness.

But then he went off to university and he changed. I wondered if he was simply adjusting to the big wide world, or if some girl had broken his heart. But he wouldn't talk, or engage beyond the minimum. You'll no doubt remember how taciturn he was whenever he came back.

It bothers me, Quinn, that I don't know what was going on in his head, or in his life back then, bothers me that we never got back the ease we had so briefly. And I don't understand his gambling and the rest.

Apologies! That's my cancer brain rambling. You know this already. What you don't know, and what I've only just realised myself, is that it also bothers me that he works for the company. He does a sterling job, but I don't know, deep down, if it's what he really wants, or if on some level he's trying to be some imagined version of Pete. I'm ashamed that I don't know the man he is inside, grieved that he's drifted so far away from me that I can't touch him any more, help him.

Which is where you come in, darling girl. If you no longer wish to take on the Lisbon hotel then I understand, but for Will's sake, I urge you to see it through. As you know, he thinks it's a terrible idea and, financially speaking, were it to be run on the lines of the current Thacker model then he would be absolutely right. Too smart by half, my youngest son! But you are also smart, and your idea for the hotel has my hearty blessing.

As you know, I wasn't thinking about

profit when I bought it. I just wanted to rescue it, challenge myself with something different. What different looks like will now be down to you and Will.

Why involve Will at all? I hear you wondering. Well, the one thing to be said for imminent death is that it makes you reflect. And, reflecting on everything, I got to thinking that tying Will to the renovation, with you by his side, might open his eyes up, stretch him in new ways, make him think about what he truly wants from life. He might even absorb some of your wondrous creativity! At the very least, he will hopefully make a dear friend in you, which is my greatest wish. And for you too, to find a true friend in him.

Your father didn't want you to be alone, Quinn, which is why he asked me to take care of you should anything ever happen to him. I have tried to do my best by you, but I must leave you now, which means that Will is all you have left of me and my family.

I know he will be angry about what I've done, but he's a good man with a good heart full of sadness. All I want for him is to rise, find peace and happiness in whatever form it comes. If I can go towards the light knowing that you've got his back, that you will help him find his own true light, then I will rest easy in my heart.

Go well, Quinn.

Your ever-loving guardian,
Anthony

CHAPTER THREE

Rossio Square, gently warm in the pale morning sunshine. And the plash-plash of the fountain was soothing, but the sweeping waves of black mosaic tile running side to side seemed to be alive, pulsing around her feet as she walked, messing with her head, which was all she needed when her poor head was already messed to the max!

That letter…

Those words…

Circling for days, tugging her every which way. Anthony had said she could forget it, live free and be happy if she thought he was wrong to have written it. He said he didn't want to burden her with his mistakes, but that was exactly what he had done! And now what was she supposed to do?

She owed him so much but—*seriously?*—helping Will find his light! Helping him when, aside from that one time, he'd never shown the slightest interest in her, made the slightest effort to get to know her, when, on the few occasions he'd actually been around her, he'd sailed wide or been curt. As for the funeral, he'd been downright rude, stepping back like that, turning away so she'd been left with her stupid hand grasping at air.

Was that what Anthony wanted for her? To be jumping through Will's hoops only to land flat on her face?

Her heart pinched. *No.* He wanted her to land on her feet smiling, with Will smiling alongside. He wanted her not to be alone, to find a friend in Will, and he wanted Will to be happy.

She dropped down onto a bench, losing herself in the sparkling froth of the fountain. All very laudable, but was it achievable? She felt a knot tightening somewhere. She wasn't up for putting herself on the line just to be dissed. Hurt. Not again, not after Liam.

She'd bent over backwards to design the right look for his café, sidelining her real clients in the process—not exactly at their pleasure—giving him her time, her skill, her advice, all so he'd feel her love. Oh, and he'd been so grateful, hadn't he? All over her like a rash, pulling her into bed, eyes aglow, saying 'I love you' over and over again. Saying it with texts. Flowers. Roses by the dozen, little cards with cupid arrows…

Her heart clenched. Some love! Because when it came to the crunch, when she had needed him, when she was tied up juggling work, and the hospice, and the shelter, too tired to see him—*sleep* with him—his love had died a sudden death. And no, maybe it wasn't great for him that she was stretched so thin, but it was worse for her, being the one who was stretched. And he knew—*knew*—that Anthony was dying, that the long hospice hours would come to an end. He could have stuck it out, supported her, for God's sake, but no. Too busy tomcatting around, finding someone else to buy roses for!

Liam was a selfish, cheating, grade-A jerk! She was well shot of him. But knowing it didn't stop the thoughts coming, the same thoughts that always came. *Why?* Why could she attract attention but never hold it? What was wrong with her? Sadie would say 'Nothing', give her the stern eye, tell her she was being too down on herself, that she rocked. But she was twenty-nine now, still rocking it single.

Oh, she'd masked up with a little feminist zeal for Will's benefit, hadn't she? Because he'd irked her, assuming she was havering about coming out here because of some guy. She'd rattled a bit of steel because she didn't want him seeing in her eyes that that was exactly her pattern: putting the boyfriend first, falling over herself to be available, not wanting whoever she was with to be deprived of her love, but also—*crucially*—not wanting to deprive herself of theirs. Living for every sweet act of intimacy, that sublime head-rush feeling of being wanted, cherished…

She bit her cheek.

Needy Quinn!

Always chasing unicorns. Was it because Mum had died just as she, Quinn, was drawing her first breath? Had she somehow sensed she was losing something irreplaceable even as she was coming into the world, so that ever since she'd been snatching at love, twisting herself to make it fit, even when it didn't?

She sighed. Who knew? And anyway, what did any of this have to do with Will? Other than that, if she couldn't convince the ones who'd at least started off liking her that she was worth sticking around for, then what chance did she have of convincing him, indifferent to her at best, that she was his friend in need?

Her heart tugged. But she owed it to Anthony to try, didn't she? Because he'd been beset with this stuff for weeks before he even wrote that letter. Guilt over Will. Going to his grave with all that heartache. How could she not feel for him now when she'd been feeling for him every day for weeks? That letter was just the grim icing on the cake, churning her up even more, so she couldn't stop thinking about it, about Pete, and Will.

Pete, the son she'd never met, the one Anthony would never talk about, but that photo on his desk spoke volumes. Pete, frozen at sixteen, tanned, tow-haired, smiling, his legs crossed, elbows on his knees, meeting the camera's eye all comfortable in his skin; Will beside him, mirroring the pose, except that his brown head was turned, tilted, looking at his brother, the adoration clearly visible on his face, his expression so sweet and open that it was impossible not to feel warmth burling, impossible not to fix on that face over and over again.

The last ever photo of the brothers together. That was what Marion, the housekeeper, had told her the day she'd found her holding the frame in her hands. Taken on holiday in France, she'd said, just weeks before Pete was knocked off his bicycle and killed.

She felt her eyes prickling, welling. Unimaginable, losing a beloved brother like that. Will had been fourteen. Fourteen, yet only weeks later, drawing strength from some hidden place Anthony didn't even know about, devastated by loss but launching himself at cracks, trying to fill the void. She swallowed hard. Rudeness aside, curt nods and miles of distance aside, she couldn't not feel for the boy Will had been. And Anthony must have known that about her, known that if he trickled in just a bit more information he could turn her to his side, hitch her to his cause.

She pressed her fingers to her eyes. *Fine!* She'd

try her best. Except, what did she have to build a friendship with Will out of? Only that one sweet moment of kindness long ago, which he was bound to have forgotten about, and that other moment in the boardroom when she'd said that stupid thing about the site visit which had made him smile.

Crinkling eyes, twinkling blue, the planes of his face turning handsome...

She felt the knot inside loosening a little. That moment had felt nice, as if they were getting along, as if they could. And he had seemed genuinely impressed about her work with the homeless. Impressed and a little bit introspective, a little bit softer. Her stomach swooped. But, of course, that was before Edward had given them their letters...

What had Anthony put in Will's letter? That he loved him, respected him, was sorry for tying him to a project he had no love for, with a partner he had no love for, but that it was for his own good? Or was it straight-up business, laying out their vision for the hotel, laying it on thick about her 'wondrous creativity', about how different this hotel was going to be from all the other Thacker hotels? Whatever it was, it was unlikely to have gone down well.

It was why she'd bailed on flying out with him, so she didn't have to sit with him on the plane, trying to make conversation, worrying about which gears were grinding away inside him. Flying out last night, staying over, had seemed like a better plan, and maybe he thought so too because when she'd called to tell him he'd sounded fine about it. Maybe he'd been faking civility, or maybe he was just relieved that he didn't have to sit with her either.

She glanced at her watch, felt her stomach swooping again. No bailing now, though. She rose, forcing her feet to walk. At least it would be easier seeing him for the first time since the will reading with Julia Levette there to act as a buffer. And who knew? Maybe when Will saw the building with his own eyes he would feel switched on, inspired. That would make everything easier.

Lisbon was such a great city after all, faded but elegant. How could Will fail to be caught up in the sight of these Pombaline buildings with their Juliet balconies? And if those didn't grab him, then maybe he'd fall for the scrum of candy-coloured buildings jostling for space on the surrounding hillsides, orange roofs fencing with the crisp blue of the March sky. Crazy pavements. Rumbling yellow trams. Warmth. Light. Life! Oh, and what about those custard tarts? To. Die. For.

She felt her step lightening, a sudden smile straining at her cheeks. Surely Will could find something to love here.

CHAPTER FOUR

'YOUR FATHER WAS lucky to get his hands on this…' Julia was running her eyes over the façade with a sort of beatific smile on her face. 'So many of these old buildings sit unclaimed for ever, all because the laws of inheritance here are so complicated.' And then she was turning, looking at him again, her smile tapering somewhat. 'I won't get on my soapbox about it, though, bore you to death.'

What to say?

He forced his lips to smile then lifted his gaze to the building, trying to seem thrilled with what he was seeing: pale gold stucco, mottled and crumbling; weathered boards where windows should have been; tufts of grass sprouting from every unfortunate crack. Right now, the word 'lucky' was not even a bottom feeder in his personal lexicon for this project. 'Ignorant', on the other hand, was headlining. Because ignorant was how he was feeling right now in front of Julia, who seemed to know so much more about

Dad's love for Lisbon and its architecture than he did, and was clearly wondering, behind her eyes, why that was.

If only Quinn was here. Oh, and the irony of that particular thought wasn't lost on him either. To think he'd been relieved when she'd said she would make her own way out. Relieved that he wouldn't have to sit beside her on the plane, making polite conversation, pretending she wasn't the spanner in his works, pretending he wasn't noticing her honey skin and the warm, floral smell of her.

Now, all he could think was that he could have used the time to grill her about the building, about what Dad was thinking, and that if he'd been able to do that then at least he would have been able to talk to Julia like a competent adult instead of standing here floundering like some prize idiot.

'Is this Quinn, coming now?'

He turned, following Julia's gaze, felt his heart catching. *There!* At the street end, coming towards them. Green coat, orange scarf, chunky black boots, not that different from his own brown ones, and those glorious dark curls, bobbing to the rhythm of her walk. He felt a smile coming, a swell of relief. Smiling because of the relief, obviously.

He looked at Julia. 'Yes, that's her.'

'Hmm.' Her eyebrows flickered. 'Anthony said she was lovely.'

His chest went tight. He didn't need Julia Levette reminding him how enamoured Dad was—*had been*—with Quinn. But he couldn't very well say nothing, could he? He was getting a vibe that Julia already thought he was a bit strange, so if he didn't declare himself a member of the Quinn Radley fan club, especially as Quinn was on his team, then the architect would likely give him another of those cryptic, assessing looks.

He geared up with a smile. 'Yeah, Quinn's great.'

Not 'lovely', because he didn't want Julia getting any fanciful notions. Of course, 'great' needed fleshing out, substantiating.

He cranked up his smile a touch. 'She has a good eye...'

Illustrate with examples, Will, to show you at least know something...

'Dad gave her one of our hub hotels to do when she was more or less straight out of college. Budget rooms—compact, you know—but she came up with some ingenious designs to make the most of the space, then styled the hell out of it so the rooms looked top class...' Sage-green walls, splashes of orange in the soft furnishings and en suite bathrooms, setting off the white bedding, adding a bit of on-point zing to the ubiquitous white bathroom suite. Green and orange! He felt a beat of recognition. She clearly had a thing for green and orange.

Julia's eyebrows lifted. 'Well, space won't be an issue here. There's nothing compact about this building.' And then she was shifting her stance, altering her demeanour, smiling a broad, welcoming smile. 'Quinn! How lovely to meet you! Are your ears burning?'

Quinn took Julia's outstretched hand in both of hers. 'Lovely to meet you too, Julia.' And then she was turning to meet his gaze, her own suddenly tentative. 'Hi, Will.'

Eyes… Lips… One corkscrew curl lighter than the rest, tumbling from a place somewhere north of her left eyebrow. But where were the words? The simple reply he'd felt rising but couldn't find now because somehow, he was flying backwards in his mind to Dad's sixtieth, seeing her in silver again, seeing her smile, her *glow*, feeling that same traitorous tug inside, that same intolerable craving.

And then it was too late. She was turning back to Julia, smiling full beam, a little chuckle in her voice. 'Why would my ears be burning?'

Julia laughed. 'Because Will's been singing your praises to the high heavens, that's why.'

Outrageous exaggeration!

'Is that right?' Her gaze came back, holding

him, turning a quizzical second into an agonising hour, and then she was smiling at Julia again, blushing a little, the way she had in the boardroom when he'd complimented her for volunteering at the homeless shelter. 'That's very nice to hear…'

He felt resistance scrambling up his walls, an urge to say that she shouldn't read anything into it, but then, just as quickly as it came, the urge was gone. So what if Quinn was surprised, flattered? She *was* a good designer, *did* have a good eye. Whatever else he felt about her, he wasn't above acknowledging that.

And hey, wasn't this what being calm and reasonable looked like, felt like? Hadn't he spent the last few days telling himself that, no matter how much it went against the grain, this was the way he had to be with Quinn now, because getting the best out of her, getting her full cooperation—aka speedy cooperation—was going to be a whole lot easier if he squashed his animosity flat and jumped through the wretched hoops Dad had set out for him.

His gut clenched. Dad had probably written as much in his letter, not that he'd read it. His desk drawer had swallowed it readily enough. Why torture himself reading Dad's justifications for hanging this crumbling albatross around his neck when reading them wasn't going to sweeten the medicine, change anything? He was encumbered. And that was all he needed to know, thank you very much.

'Right…' Julia was bending to a bag by her feet, pulling out hard hats, handing them over. 'Not very fashionable, I'm afraid, but we need to comply.'

'Because these are obviously going to save us if the roof caves in!' Quinn's eyes came to his briefly, full of mischievous light.

He felt an answering smile twitching, a little glow of camaraderie. The hard hat thing always mystified him too.

'Now, now, Quinn.' Julia was giving Quinn the stern eye, pulling a fat door key out of her pocket. 'There's no chance of the roof caving in. We got as far as supporting it, making it safe, before…' Her eyes came to his, softening with an apology for skimming so close to the bone, he supposed. 'Before we put everything on hold.' She drew a clearing breath. 'But the hat will save you from any loose debris dislodged by birds and so on, so it's wise to wear it, as well as being mandatory. Oh, and while we're on the subject of safety, please don't wander off when we're inside. The building is hazardous in places.'

'I was only joking about the hat…' Quinn was placating now, plonking her hat on, reaching round to tighten it. And then her gaze caught his, catching alight, emptying his lungs. 'Come on, Will. Get with the programme!'

The programme. The renovation.

The push and pull of Quinn. Eyes… Lips… Smile…

He lifted his hat, ramming it on hard, feeling the awkward grip of it, the stiff spring of its straps. How to breathe? How to think straight? He ground his jaw. Losing time every time she looked at him wasn't what he'd expected, bargained for. He didn't want this. Didn't like it.

Oh, God!

How was he going to get through this day?

Wrought-iron balusters. Mahogany rail, splitting in places but, in the right hands, not beyond redemption. She snapped a few pictures then lowered her phone, fighting a shiver as she ran her eyes around the damp-mottled walls of the stairwell. These abandoned buildings were always dank, uniquely bone-chilling, but once the roof was fixed and the building was watertight again, there was nothing here that couldn't be made good…

'Quinn?'

Will!

Concern in his voice. *Irritation.* Her heart seized. Irritation because she was doing her usual, wasn't she? Getting so caught up in light, and texture, and potential, that she'd inadvertently left him alone with Julia.

Poor Will!

Out of his depth with the architect, with this entire project. Ever since they'd come inside he'd been deferring to her, relying on her to broker the discussion, but she needed to take pictures because he was in a hurry, talking about doing things piecemeal. Maybe that wouldn't be possible in the end, but if she didn't have the reference material to work with then it definitely wouldn't be.

She clapped a hand to her hat and leaned over the balustrade. There he was, looking up from the ground floor, his face pale in the light spilling from the skylight window above. His throat was pale too, the portion of it she could see above the collar of his dark shirt. Dark shirt, grey herringbone coat. He looked good. But then Will always did, whatever he was wearing.

Jeans and tee shirts on those rare summer days he'd been home from uni, before he'd taken himself off to some other, better place…that chunky blue sweater he'd worn the Christmas they'd all gone to the pub for the quiz. His thick brown hair had been longer then, damply tousled from the falling snow they'd ploughed through to get there. *Strange…* Talking to Anthony on the way there, but on the way home silent… She blinked. Why was she even thinking about that?

'Hey!' She switched on a smile, beaming it at him. 'What is it?'

His brows crimped. 'Are you coming, or what?'

Imperious tone.

She laced her own tone with deliberate sweetness. 'Yes, when I've finished what I'm doing.'

He made a little impatient noise. 'What *are* you doing?'

She held her phone out. 'Taking pictures, videos. Making notes. I can't keep everything in my head.'

'Oh.' His expression relaxed a little. 'Sorry. I didn't know.' And then his face disappeared, and the stairwell filled with the sound of his leaping boots. Elongated intervals—two treads at a time. And then he was arriving, thrusting his hands into his coat pockets as if he needed something to do, as if now that he was here he didn't quite know what to say.

She felt her heart giving. Impossible not to feel for him. Out of his depth with Julia. Out of his depth with her too, but standing here all the same, looking awkward, endearingly vulnerable. She could feel softness stirring, as it had outside when Julia said he'd been singing her praises. Same look in his eyes now as then. Resistant, but porous somehow.

But she couldn't say anything, couldn't make an overture without a definite 'in'. Besides, the last time she'd tried he'd dissed her. Once bitten and all that. So, it was a case of pretending to be oblivious to the whole running up two flights of stairs thing, pretending that the only thought in her head, the only possible topic of conversation, was the building.

She smiled. 'I'm sorry it's taking a while. It's just a long way to come back if I find I've missed something.'

He shook his head. 'Don't apologise.' And then his mouth stiffened. 'I'm just...'

Floundering. Grieving. Did he even know he was? Was he able to admit it to himself? She felt a beat of indecision, but only a beat.

'I know.'

His eyes flared briefly, then softened a little.

Relief swept through. Any kind of softness was good and infinitely better than the cold shoulder she'd got at the funeral.

And then, as if he wanted to shake the moment off, he was moving across the landing, lifting his gaze to the skylight. 'If you do need to come back though, just come. As often as you need. On the company, obviously.'

'Anything to speed things up, huh?'

'Yes.' His eyes came back. 'As long as your own schedule permits, of course.'

'Oh, of course.' She raised her eyebrows at him, so he'd know that she'd caught the all too obvious afterthought.

And then suddenly, unexpectedly, he smiled. A warm smile that creased his cheeks, lifting his face into the realm of drop-dead gorgeous. 'I like that I don't have to pretend with you, Quinn.'

Mediterranean blue eyes. Eyes that could easily stop a heart, catch a breath out, make a voice struggle to form a word.

She swallowed. 'Pretend?'

He shrugged. 'You know how I feel about this project, know that I want to hatch and dispatch it ASAP.' His voice dipped low. 'Julia isn't in the picture, and I don't want to let on. I sense she'd be affronted if she knew how much I *don't* love this building.'

Her heart fell. It was good that he was confiding in her, definitely a step in the right direction, but what he was confiding wasn't. He wasn't seeing the good as she'd hoped, feeling inspired. And his expression was only soft right now because she wasn't Julia, someone he had to pretend with. Her heart paused.

Then again, that he was up here talking to her like this was something, wasn't it? She felt a tingle. Okay, so maybe the waves weren't parting for him on the building front, but there were other fronts, the main one being that, after years of more or less ignoring her, he had just vaulted up two flights to talk to her. That was progress. The kind of progress she could put to good use…

She shot him a smile, going with a conspiratorial tone. 'Where is Julia, by the way?'

'On a phone call.'

'Ah…' So she had a bit of time to dip a toe in the water, see how cold it was.

She lifted her phone to seem semi-preoccupied, framed a shot. 'Well, I suppose the building *is* quite hard to love at the moment…' She tapped the screen, then looked up and around, sighing for effect. 'Of course, damp's a killer, makes everything seem so hopeless. It can be hard to see past it…'

'Oh, here we go. You're about to tell me you can, aren't you?'

Challenging gaze. Wry smile.

She felt a smile of her own stirring. He might have rumbled her, but she could roll with it.

'Well, of course! I mean, I wouldn't be much good at my job if I couldn't see my way through this stuff.'

'And you think, what? That if you sprinkle your fairy dust I'm suddenly going to fall in love with this crumbling pile, leap about with enthusiasm?' His eyebrows went up. 'Sorry to disappoint you, but that's not going to happen.'

She felt a 'Why?' rising but bit it back. They

weren't close enough for whys yet. Better to go with humour.

She slid her own eyebrows up. 'I wasn't expecting instant results, to be honest.'

Something ruffled the surface of his gaze momentarily and then a sheepish smile softened his features. 'Just as well, since I have nothing in the creative vision department.' His eyes made a quick, hopeless sweep of the landing. 'I look around and all I can see is a massive headache.' And then he was moving over to the wall, running his fingers over a bad section, setting off a small avalanche of loose plaster. 'Case in point.' His eyes came back, half triumphant, half despairing. 'I see a crumbling wall and after that it's all panic and white noise in my head. What do you see?'

She felt tenderness blooming in her chest. His honesty was disarming. As for fairy dust—pointless. What Will needed to banish his white noise was information.

She rooted a pen out of her pocket then went over to join him by the wall, digging the nib into the plaster, raddling it backwards and forwards to loosen it, scraping off a small section until the underlying masonry was visible.

'What I see are solid walls with areas of loose plaster—plaster that can be knocked off and redone. It's not a problem.'

Bemusement in his eyes, and interest, which could only be a good sign. Whatever she did, she mustn't stop talking.

'Now, if the supporting walls were crumbling then that would be a headache, but the bones of this building seem good to me. It just needs a little TLC.'

'TLC? Is that right?' He put his hands to his mouth, mimicking a loudhailer. 'Understatement alert!'

She couldn't hold in a chuckle. 'Okay, a lot of TLC. But there's plenty of good stuff.' She felt her heart rising, a ball of enthusiasm starting to roll. She set off along the corridor, touching a door frame. 'These frames are still good, and most of the doors are too.' She turned, walking backwards so she could see his face, judge his reaction to what she was saying. 'The stair balusters are wrought iron so they only need a clean, and the rail might look ropey right now, but it's mahogany so it'll refurbish a treat.'

'I'll buy that.' He was following now, his mouth twisting into a reluctant but twinkly smile. 'I'll go so far as to say I'm pleased because it sounds quick.'

She felt mischief sparking. 'Well, at least you're pleased about something!'

His eyes flashed. 'I have my moments.'

Smiling moments. Twinkly moments. *All good!*

She looked up at the broken, elegant ceiling. This was going to be a harder sell, but she had to try. She licked her lips, steeling herself. 'On the downside, restoring this ornate plasterwork won't be speedy. It's going to need a specialist, but it'll be worth it because—'

'Quinn, stop!'

Loud eyes. Contorting face. Some kind of horror…

Her heart lurched. 'What?'

His hand shot out, stretching into the void between them. 'Don't move—'

But she couldn't not move because her back foot was already descending, going down, down into…

Oh, God!

Nothing. Air instead of floor. And then everything was tilting, rushing in, out, spinning past, ceiling, plaster, her own hands clawing at frantic air and then somehow, *somehow*, Will was there, seizing her elbows, yanking her hard against him as he launched himself backwards, dragging her clear.

Cripes! He was breathing hard, panting warm gusts into her hair. 'Are you okay?'

Was she? She was shaking all over. *Vibrating.* She could feel her heart banging against her ribs, banging against his chest, but banging was beating, and beating was good. Beating meant she was alive. Alive, and in his arms—his, of all people's—being held tight, so tight and close that she could smell the warm, lingering trace of soap or shower gel, or maybe it was cologne. *Whatever!*

Why was she even noticing that? The scent of him, the way he was just the right height. *For what?* Why, when her head was still reeling, was it running off on stupid tangents, coming up with insane ideas, such as how good it would feel to snuggle in closer and stay there, just breathing, feeling close and warm, feeling safe, feeling—

'Quinn…?' He straightened suddenly, leaning back to look at her. 'Are you okay?'

Concern in his eyes, kindness, turning the air soft, filling it with some sweet, tugging charge.

She nodded. 'Yes. Thanks to you.'

He shook his head minutely, as if he didn't want to hear it, but why wouldn't he want to? He'd saved her from an almighty tumble. Her stomach dived. Or something worse.

She checked in, taking inventory. No hat, no phone. Fallen, dropped—lost. Without her even noticing. A blind second…a broken link. A gap in her memory. And then the world was trying to tilt, or maybe it was her head reeling again. She forced herself to breathe, reconnect with his gaze.

'Will, what happened?'

His eyes held hers for a beat, then his features set hard. 'Oh, nothing much. Just a minor, complete absence of floor.'

She blinked. 'What?'

But before he could answer she was moving, twisting out of his arms, turning to look back along the corridor. For a long second, she was silent, taking in the sight he almost hadn't seen himself, wouldn't have seen at all if he'd been remotely interested in the dilapidated ceiling. A hole. Four floorboards wide, its edges rotted and crumbling.

'Oh, my God.' Her body seemed to deflate and then she was turning round again, her voice close to a whisper. 'You're right.' Her eyes flickered, taking a moment to settle on his. 'Complete absence…'

The state of her… Ashen-faced. Shock beating behind her lovely eyes. His heart kicked. Why the hell hadn't this wretched building been checked for safety before their visit? All very well dishing out safety helmets—which, by the way, seemed to come off far too easily—but what about the fricking floorboards, actual holes that people—*Quinn*—could fall through? If he hadn't been here…

His heart kicked again, nailing him in the

stomach this time. If he hadn't been here, spreading his gloom about, she would never have been walking backwards in the first place, trying to enthuse him, get him to see the good. He felt his insides shrivelling, his mouth drying to dust. This was all his fault.

'Thank you, Will…' Her hand was on his arm, squeezing gently, warmth in her gaze, pouring out gratitude he didn't deserve. 'If you hadn't been here…'

'Don't.' He swallowed hard, removing her hand as gently as he could manage. 'If I hadn't been here, you wouldn't have been anywhere near that hole.'

She let out an incredulous breath. 'Hang on a minute.' Her eyes were striking up, pinning him. 'You're not blaming yourself for this, are you?'

'Who else? If you hadn't been trying to get me onside—'

'I'd have still walked along here, eyes on the ceiling, taking photos…' She was shaking her head at him, frustration brimming. 'It's what I *do*, Will. All the time. I get distracted, caught up in what I'm doing.' Her lips pressed together, tight with impatience. 'If you knew me at all then you would know that about me, know that I'm not just saying it. This time it was the staircase, the stairwell. I was walking up, taking pictures—thinking about the space, what I could do—and, before I knew it, I was on this floor and then you came…' She shrugged, sighed. 'But if you hadn't I'd have carried on, blazing my own ill-advised trail.'

He felt his heart cramping. Why was she doing this, trying to make him feel better? She owed him nothing. Especially after the unforgivable way he'd behaved towards her at Dad's funeral. And feeling guilty about it straight afterwards, *still* feeling guilty, didn't make him a good person.

But she was good through and through. Oh, he didn't know her, no, but he could feel her, the sweetness in her, the warmth. He'd always been able to feel it. It was why he'd tried to reach out to her when she'd first arrived at the house, because he could see what she was, couldn't bear that she was hurting and alone. Even Dad had succumbed, hadn't he? Let Quinn run through him like a hot knife through butter, bringing out his hidden sides. Dad, who hadn't been given to warmth, letting his hair down, smiling. Dad who'd made hard work of everything except, ironically, work itself.

Making hard work of things. As he did. *Was* doing right now. Whoa! Was he turning into Dad? Resistant. Armoured. Or was he there already, stiffly cast in the old man's mould? No more the open-hearted eighteen-year-old he'd once been but thirty-one and calcified.

He touched his face. Hadn't he felt these muscles rebelling just minutes ago when she'd made him smile? Jaw cracking, pain blooming. The price of a smile. The price of being Will Thacker. Oh, he might have been sticking to the script he'd written for himself, to make nice with Quinn for the sake of the project so she would roll things along quickly, but fact was, deep down, he was still fighting it tooth and nail, wasn't he? Setting his face against it so hard that she was having to sing for her supper, work to drag a shred of interest out of him, and that wasn't fair, wasn't right. His heart pulsed. See how it had nearly ended.

He lowered his hand, drew her back into focus. He had to do better, apply himself properly. Not for Dad's sake, but for hers. He inhaled deep into his lungs. It wasn't as if he didn't have the skills. No, he couldn't see through crumbling plaster, but he knew how to bring a project in, and yes, renovating a building was different to developing a new site, but it all boiled down to planning, budgeting, managing, which were definitely his bag. So, no more making things hard, for himself or for her. Especially her. He set his lips. And he wasn't letting her take the blame for what had happened either.

'I'm not buying it, Quinn.' Her chin lifted in

a gesture of defiance, but that was all right. He was feeling sure-footed now, lighter somehow. 'I think you'd have stopped at the head of the stairs, looked around, then gone back down because, whatever you say about getting caught up, I think you'd have been mindful that we'd be wondering where you were.' He opened his palms to push the point. 'So you see, my fault.'

Her brow pleated. 'Are we still arguing about this?'

'Absolutely.'

Her gaze tightened on his, as if she thought she could make him fold with her eyes, and then she was puffing her cheeks out, giving up.

'Well, you're right about one thing. I do try to be mindful.' Her eyes flashed. 'But I'm also right because I do get distracted...' She frowned, considering for a moment, and then her eyes brightened. 'Why don't we go halves?'

Sharing the blame. Not as convivial as sharing a pizza—which he could totally murder right now—but it was something. Better than stringing this out anyway, which was the likely alternative since she seemed to be as stubborn as he was. Besides, wasn't working together all about compromise?

'Okay.' He sighed, labouring it to make it seem like he wasn't a pushover. 'If you insist. We can split it.'

'Cool.' She beamed a triumphant smile but then suddenly her gaze stilled. 'We're going to have to zip it too because I just remembered what Julia said outside...'

'About what?'

'About *not* wandering off.'

'Ahh!' How could he have forgotten? And Julia was bound to be off the phone any second, wondering where they were. He felt a flick of schoolboy panic. 'We should go down.'

She nodded. 'Yeah...' But then, incredibly, she was turning in the opposite direction. 'I'll just get my hat and my phone...'

What?

He grabbed her arm. 'No, you don't!'

Her eyes filled with bemusement. 'I was *obviously* going to be careful.'

'You're not going to *be* anything, Quinn! And you're not going anywhere near that hole either.' He squeezed her arm to make her stay. 'I'll get them.'

Something flickered through her gaze—surprise perhaps, gratitude, maybe a combo of the two, and then she broke into a smile that split his atom. 'Thanks, Will.'

'No problem...' Unlike breathing. Functioning. He cut free and scanned the floor ahead, glad of the distraction.

There, against the wall beside the lethal chasm,

one white hat. One phone in its—*surprise, surprise*—orange case.

He went to the wall, flattening himself against it, testing the floor with his foot between each sideways step.

Wasn't today just the gift that kept on giving? Confusion at every turn. Warm, golden feelings he had no idea what to do with. And now here he was, risking life and limb for a hat and a phone because they were hers. Of all people, hers!

'Be careful, Will...'

He paused. Her concern was touching though. He bent his knees, scooping up the hat. 'What do you think I'm being?'

'I just...' And then she made a noise that sounded suspiciously like a giggle being smothered.

Was he amusing now? He planted his foot, ducking a second time for her phone. To be fair, he probably did look like a bit of a berk, inching along like this in his smart overcoat and safety helmet!

When he got back, she was smiling at him hard. 'You were amazing!'

Definitely laughing at him, but that was fine. He could deal with that.

He pressed his lips together, nodding. 'I know. I was actually thinking the same thing.'

Her face stretched. 'Oh, and so modest!'

He nodded again. 'That too.'

She stared at him for a blink, and then suddenly she was laughing into his eyes, making the warm golden stuff flow again. What was she doing to him? Making him want to be funny, making him feel…

Focus!

He held out her things. 'Here you go.'

'Thanks.' She took them, holding his gaze for a sweet, tangled beat, and then she was jamming on the hat, brushing her phone off, tapping the screen to life. 'Oh, thank goodness.' And then she was looking up again, her eyes twinkling like magic. 'After all your heroics, I'd have been gutted if it was broken!'

CHAPTER FIVE

WILL DIPPED HIS CHIN. 'So, you've got trades primed, ready to go?'

Julia nodded. 'More or less.'

Impossible not to look at him—to *stare!* He was so different. Ever since they had rejoined Julia—ambling back through as if they had only been in the adjoining room waiting for her to finish on the phone—Will had been shouldering the load, taking notes, displaying the smarts Anthony used to so admire.

'What about specialist plasterers?' His eyes came to hers briefly, stirring a warm little ripple inside. 'I'm informed that restoring plasterwork can take a while.'

'It can, but I have a team lined up. They could start in a couple of months.'

'No earlier?'

Focus, Quinn!

She cut in. 'Will…' His gaze came back. Warm. Disconcertingly attentive. 'A month isn't going to affect the time schedule on a project like this.

If the other trades are starting soon, it would be better to hold off on the restoration plasterers because they're going to need scaffold towers erecting and those will only hinder access for the other trades, slowing them down.' She smiled to soften the blow. 'No point robbing Peter to pay Paul.'

His eyes signalled resignation. 'Okay.' And then he was turning back to Julia. 'I suppose we need to prioritise the roof anyway.' His lips moved as if to smile, then flattened into a line. 'And the floors too, for safety.'

Her heart quivered. Upstairs… Pulling her from the brink… Holding her tight, breathing into her hair. That close, safe feeling. Then arguing with her about whose fault it was that she'd almost taken the express route to the floor below. Blaming himself for making her work at getting him onside when it wasn't he who'd asked her to do that at all, but his father.

And yes, she might well have stumbled down a hole anyway, because she *did* get distracted, but she'd been walking backwards upstairs expressly because of Anthony, because she'd been thinking about what *he* wanted her to do for Will—stretching Will's horizons—and of course Anthony meant well, wanting her to open Will up, but many a slip and all that. Like at that pub quiz…

Her heart pulsed. Oh, it was all coming back

now: Anthony asking Will if he'd mind joining that other table because some friend of his had pitched up and wanted to join them… Will smiling, getting up. But it had felt a bit off to her, made her heart hurt for Will, and maybe it had made Will hurt as well because he'd been silent all the way home.

Typical Anthony! Blinkered once he'd got a notion in his head. Maybe it was a strength in business, but it didn't work for family, for Will. And he'd come to see it too late, hadn't he? Regretted it too late.

She drew Will back into focus. But she couldn't get into all that with him. Not yet. For now, she was just glad they had 'upstairs'—the saving part, and the funny part when he'd gone back for her stuff—because it was their secret now, a warm little strip of connection between them that was making everything feel better, more hopeful.

'So, you're saying all new pantiles?' Will was frowning now, tapping calculations into his phone.

Julia shrugged. 'If you want to turn this around quickly then new is the best option. Reclaimed materials take time to source.'

'And what's the lead time on new?'

She held in a smile. He was relentless. Even the über-serene and consummately professional Julia was beginning to look a fraction jaded.

'I'll have to check with Filipe.' And then Julia's gaze was moving, flitting between them. 'That's Filipe Alexandre. He'll be your project manager. He's very good, speaks excellent English.' She riffled in her bag, producing two white business cards which she handed over. 'Filipe's details. If you have any questions about trades, materials or scheduling, he's your guy.' She smiled. 'I'll call him later, give him the green light, then I'll touch base with you again next week, let you know when the trades are starting.' And then suddenly she shuddered. 'God, it's cold in here. We should have taken this to a café or something.'

'We can still do that.' Will looked over, checking in, then shot Julia an eager smile. 'What about lunch? We could all go grab a bite…'

Julia pulled a disappointed face. 'Oh, I'd have loved that, but I've got another meeting, so we'll have to call it a day.' She frisked her hands together. 'Unless you've got more to do, in which case I'll give you the key and you can drop it off at my office later.'

Will looked over. 'Have you got everything you need?'

'Absolutely…' She felt an icy shiver tangling with her spine. 'I'm actually freezing as well.'

He smiled then looked at Julia. 'Decision made. We're leaving.'

* * *

Quinn opened her coat then tipped her head back, closing her eyes. 'Oh, this is heavenly…'

He felt a smile tugging at his lips. 'You're easily pleased.'

Because they were nowhere yet. Just outside on the cobbled pavement, minus Julia, who'd whizzed off in her little car moments ago.

'What's not to be pleased about?' She fanned her coat out wider, smiling blindly at the sky. 'It's gorgeous out here.'

Bang on, but not for the reason she was thinking! He shut his eyes to stop them staring at her. Staring was a new problem, along with breathing. And his pizza pangs were getting to be a problem. But what were a few more starving minutes if Quinn wanted to make like a lizard on a rock?

He inhaled, letting the warm dry air cycle through his lungs. Definitely nicer out here than inside. Of course, as Julia said, once the boards came off the windows and the roof was sorted, the whole place would feel different—lighter, airier. Even he could almost imagine it…

'You've got hat hair!'

He opened his eyes.

Quinn was looking at him, holding in a smile rather badly.

Was he really so comical? He felt the air softening. He used to be, didn't he? Around Pete anyway. Pete had brought it out in him. And he'd brought it out in Pete. Mum used to say they were like a pair of flints sparking. His heart caught. A pair reduced to one. As much use as one hand clapping. But now Quinn was looking at him the way Pete used to, hanging on the edge of a smile, and he could feel that vital spark jumping again, an irresistible light rising. So, he had hat hair? Well, he could work with that!

He bent over, raking at his hair until he could feel it standing on end, then straightened, meeting her gaze. 'Better?'

She made a satisfying little snorting noise. 'Erm…'

He felt his cheeks creasing, an enjoyable chuckle rumbling. 'Too much?'

Her eyes narrowed by a playful margin. 'Just a touch.' And then she was smiling full beam, twisting her hands together as if she was itching to sort him out.

He would only have to drop his arms, offer up a hopeless little shrug, and those hands would involve themselves in his hair, he could tell. Smoothing him out, fingers softly teasing, but that would be…he felt his head trying to swim…also too much. Off the scale. Especially after what had happened earlier. Hard enough even before that, staying level around her, but afterwards—*ever since*—he'd been going full tilt trying not to remember her warm skin smell and how it had felt to hold her close, to feel the spiralling softness of her hair against his face. If she hadn't twisted free…

He smiled to reset, dealing with his hair himself, talking on as if he hadn't just been thinking what he'd been thinking. 'By the way, in case you're wondering, you don't have hat hair…'

She laughed, winding a finger into her curls. 'Oh, the hat hasn't been invented yet that could stand a chance with mine!' And then her eyes were sweeping over him, approving, softening into his. 'You've got it now…'

And there his breath went again, catching.

Her head tilted. 'You look very smart.'

Which sounded like a cue, a way to move things along so that he wasn't dangling here at the mercy of her amber gaze, losing his breath and most of his wits.

He smiled. 'Smart enough for an outdoor table somewhere?'

Her face split. 'Definitely! It's been a million years since breakfast.'

And, just like that, he was thinking of a tease, wanting to be funny for her, wanting to make her eyes glow and twinkle, which was stupid—*self-defeating*—because her eyes were the problem, and her smile, and the way her cheeks lifted, dimpling. Making that happen was only going to tangle him up again. But he couldn't help it, couldn't switch off the desire to see himself reflected in her smiling eyes.

He slid his eyebrows up. 'Would that be a million years on this planet, or in some other universe?'

Her gaze solidified. 'Very funny!' And then she was starting along the street, laughing, drawing him along in her slipstream, blinding him with her light. 'When you know me better, you'll know that as well as getting caught up in things, I'm rather prone to hyperbole.'

'That's some view!' Will was sipping his beer, gazing out over the sweep of the city.

She wanted to agree but speaking would draw his gaze back to her and then she would blush, because the view she was busy appreciating was him. His lovely profile: that fine, straight nose, that sweet, full mouth, that lovely thick brown hair lifting off his forehead in the faint breeze. He was just in his shirtsleeves now, rolled back, because slogging up to this terrace restaurant had proved too much in a coat. All through lunch, she'd had to stop her eyes from sliding to his shoulders, his chest, his arms. But now that his gaze was otherwise occupied, her eyes were running amok, taking in his contours, the sprinkle of dark hair on his thick forearms—arms that had pulled her from the brink, held her tight.

'What did you say the square down there was called?' He turned, putting his glass down, and then his eyes were lifting, locking onto hers.

She swallowed. 'Rossio. Although it's really King Pedro the Fourth Square. He's the poor soul stuck on top of the column.' Which maybe she shouldn't have mentioned, because Pedro was Portuguese for Peter, wasn't it? She felt her chest tightening. She'd never said Pete's name to Will before, had never heard him say it either. Was he making the connection? Maybe if she just kept talking…

She picked up her glass, sipping quickly. '*Rossio* is roughly equivalent to our English word "common", as in common land. Back in the day, it was where the executions happened.'

'Nice.' His eyes flickered, without a trace of Pete, thank God, and then his gaze narrowed a little. 'How do you know all this?'

What to say?

She didn't want to upend him now—upset him—not when they were getting on so well, having actual fun, when he seemed to be stepping up on the project front, albeit still in a tearing hurry. Pace was going to be a hurdle, not one she wanted to face yet, not when he was proving such a sweet surprise, messing his hair up like that to look like a scarecrow! She felt warmth unfurling. In a million years she'd never have guessed he could be so slapstick, so completely adorable.

But she couldn't let the sunshine, and the wine, and his ocean eyes lull her into La-La Land. Anthony had wanted her to help him find his light, and she couldn't do that without touching the dark, without ever mentioning his father.

She set her glass down, bracing a little. 'Your dad told me.'

Something moved behind his eyes, but he wasn't turning his face away, which was good.

'As you know, he liked talking about Lisbon. I guess some of it stuck…'

His lips tightened. 'Right.'

Was that resistance starting? She dug in. No way was she losing him now. 'There's nothing like seeing it for real, though.' She aimed a smile into his eyes. 'I was out first thing this morning, walking…'

Empty streets. Pale sun. Sky turning blue.

His features softened. 'Sounds like a nice thing to do.'

She felt a flick of relief and, in the same beat, a spark igniting. 'It was so quiet, Will. Mellow. Or maybe it just felt like that because it's warmer here than it is in London right now and the pavements really *are* golden.'

He smiled, then turned to the view. 'Incredibly, it's my first time here.'

Because of Anthony's love for the place, he meant. She felt her heart lifting. Maybe it was only an oblique nod to his father, but it felt like a milestone, a tiptoe step towards a possible future conversation with him about Anthony, and everything that went with that. For now, she was glad of this new thing they had in common.

'It's my first time here too.'

His gaze swung back. 'Really? I assumed...' His lips pressed together. 'I mean, the way you led us up to this place...'

'No, I saw it earlier from down there, that's all. Thought it might be worth a try.'

'Hmm.' And then he broke a smile. 'You've clearly got a good radar for pizza.'

'Honed over many years!'

He chuckled and then his gaze settled. 'So, what else did you see?'

Interest in his eyes, irresistible warmth.

She felt a fresh smile surging. 'I saw—walked down—Rua Augusta. It's one of the main drags, pedestrianised, very pleasant. There's a massive arch at the end, the Arco da Rua Augusta, which leads into a vast square, and beyond that, literally across the road, is the river.'

'The Tagus?'

Raised, earnest eyebrows.

She felt her lips curving, her heart dancing. 'Apparently so.'

His eyes smiled back, crinkling. Crinkling her breath, her focus.

She picked up her glass to reset. 'I stayed there for a while, then came back up another street and stumbled upon the Santa Justa lift—which I still can't get over!'

He shook his head. 'Me neither.' And then he was turning to look over the rail. 'It's a weird-looking thing, isn't it?'

She followed his gaze, feeling the little heart dip that happened every time she looked at the grey iron tower with its great boxy top that didn't fit at all with the terracotta roofs around it.

His eyebrows drew in. 'Incongruous, but oddly compelling.' And then his eyes found hers. 'Did you go up it?'

'Heavens, no! It gives me the heebie-jeebies.'

He pulled a sheepish face. 'Not just me then?'

She felt a warm rush of fellow feeling, then yet another smile coming. 'No, not just you. I had a quick look then walked up to Rossio Square, which has these insane waves of mosaic running side to side. You can't really see them from here but, trust me, they make you feel tipsy when you're walking across, even when you've only had coffee!'

'Sounds awful.'

But his eyes were smiling, twinkling into hers, making her heart soar. How was this turning out to be so easy? All those years of distance, and now they were flowing together, mingling like tides.

She smiled. 'Not *awful*. Just weird—but in a fun way.'

'I'm sold!' He grinned, then he was turning, looking down at the square again, his voice shading towards wistfulness. 'I wish I could have…'

She held her breath. Was he about to say something about Anthony, that he wished he could have come here with him? That would be a breakthrough, would open things right up…

But then suddenly his features were darkening, hardening, his whole demeanour changing. When he turned back to look at her, his gaze was cool, bordering on disdainful.

'Is that why you came over by yourself last night, Quinn?' His eyebrows arched in a blatant challenge. 'So you could hit the streets first thing, get some *exploring* under your belt?'

Her lungs emptied. What was he doing? Saying? Why was he looking at her like this? She felt maddening tears prickling, her shoulders starting to blaze. And why was he even asking when his tone said it all, that he knew it wasn't the reason? He was poking her deliberately.

Why? When they'd been getting on so well,

having fun, for goodness' sake! Was it a trust thing, some kind of bizarre honesty test? Did he want to hear her say: No, I came last night so I didn't have to sit with you on the plane, wondering what the hell to say to you, wondering what Anthony put in your letter? Was that it?

She swallowed, paddling hard. Well, if he wanted to know, then she could say that, minus the letter part. Getting into that… She baulked. Too many unknowns! Besides, she couldn't risk him asking her about her own letter, all that *leading him to the light* business…

She inhaled carefully. But the rest was fine, maybe even desirable, because what was the point of trying to be friends with him if she couldn't be honest with him about herself? Fears. Feelings. Steering clear of Anthony, and Anthony's letter, was one thing, but his question—however barbed, however oblique, concerned the two of them, and it was true there was now, somehow, such a thing as the 'two of them', however new, however fragile, and this new, fragile thing would never grow, never flourish if she sidestepped this, let it wither her. So…

She set her glass down, then fastened her eyes on his. 'No, that wasn't the reason, Will…' *breathe* '…I just thought it would be easier on both of us if we met at the building, given that the last time we saw each other was at the reading of the will.'

His lips parted, and then something seemed to shift behind his gaze, absorbing his attention. Was he going back, replaying it in his mind? Ranting at Edward. Glaring at her through the glass. Trying to unhook her from the project, getting slapped down for it by Edward. Talking about piecemeal and dovetailing for speed. Then softening. Chuckling over her dumb site visit question. Praising her for her voluntary work. Her heart caught. And then it had been the letters, the soft rasp of those envelopes sliding over the table, the colour draining from Will's face...

She shook herself. 'I thought if we had the building to focus on, and Julia with us, then it would give us a chance to acclimatise, to start afresh.'

'Right.' His gaze held her distant for a long, unsmiling second, and then he was draining his glass, putting it down again with an air of finality. 'We should go. We don't want to miss our flight.'

Just like that! Without comment, without feeling! Cutting her off—effectively.! She felt a knife twisting somewhere. It was the funeral all over again, the same hot prickle playing with her spine, bothering her eyes, same stupid hand left grasping at air. Was this how it was going to be with him? Hot. Cold. Up. Down.

She reached for her things, swallowing a sob. To think she'd been enjoying his company. Relishing the sweet surprise of him, the way his eyes could twinkle all warm, the stupid things they had in common: a passion for thin crust pizza and a vague unease about the grey, neo-gothic structure that was the Elevador de Santa Justa! Relishing him, tingling inside because of him when, all this time, he'd been saving his biggest surprise for last, this cruel trick up his sleeve, this talent for turning light to dark in a heartbeat, fire to ice.

She bit into her lip hard. Well, she'd learned her lesson. No more opening up so he could shut her down. No more flying her hopes high for him to just cut loose. She stared into the depths of her tote, breathing through.

For Anthony's sake, she couldn't give up on him, but she wasn't setting herself up for another fall either. She'd done it with Liam, helping him, getting nothing of worth back. And no, Will wasn't her boyfriend and she definitely didn't love him, but for some reason he had the power to hurt her, and she hadn't signed up for being trampled on, dissed, put through the mill. She wasn't standing for it, and he was going to know all about it!

'Quinn…'

She looked up. He was on his feet now, gesturing for her to come, a slight, polite smile fixed on his face.

She felt a knot yanking tight in her chest, a furious surge of rippling energy. She pushed up from her chair, switching on the brightest, widest smile she could muster just for the sheer pleasure of knocking his paltry effort clean off the wicket.

'Chillax, Will. I'm coming.'

CHAPTER SIX

'HEY, WILL THACKER...' Catherine's voice slid into his ear from behind and then she appeared beside him, her long blonde hair swinging. 'What are you doing after?'

Code for: do you want to invite me back to your place and take my clothes off? A month ago, he might have called a cab, taken her home, but now he could feel his stomach turning at the thought. Not that she wasn't attractive. He just wasn't interested, couldn't imagine being so ever again.

He shucked the ice in his glass. 'I'm going home.'

'Aww, darling.' She flicked a glance at the tables. 'Did you have a bad night with Mr Blackjack?' Her fingers connected with his nape, stroking. 'I could take your mind off it.'

He reached up, removing her hand, smiling to soften whatever level of blow it might be to her. 'No thanks, I'm good.'

'Aww, Will...'

She was leaning away now, pouting, contriving to look hurt, but she was way off the mark because hurt didn't look like that. Real hurt, jugular deep hurt, was what he had seen welling in Quinn's eyes, what he had inflicted on her, all because he'd lost the plot. And now he couldn't stop seeing her eyes, feeling her pain, feeling it twisting inside him with all the crushing guilt and remorse. And he couldn't stop replaying the way she had left him at the airport—that scant goodbye then striding off through the barriers without a backward glance—because replaying it hurt and he deserved to hurt, deserved to feel that knife twisting over and over again.

'Why don't you have a drink with me, Will?'

Catherine! Still looking at him, still flirting. *Why?* Couldn't she read him at all?

He shrugged. 'Because I don't want to.' He downed the last of his drink and got up, battling a sudden hot swell of emotion. 'I'm sorry, but can't you see? I'm done here.'

He drew in a steadying breath. So that didn't work, didn't take his mind off anything. He couldn't focus on the cards long enough to count them, and Catherine wasn't Quinn.

Not even close...

He flicked up his collar, aimed a nod at the doorman and set off walking. *Quinn...* Hanging on the edge of a smile, waiting for him to be funny. Looking at him the way Pete used to, drawing the clown out of him like Pete used to, putting little pieces of his old self back. The happy pieces. The light-as-air pieces. Making him feel how he used to feel before the mirror cracked. And more besides. Feeling her warmth flowing, that sweet, tingling connection. Losing himself in her smile, in her gaze, in the way her lips sipped wine from a glass…

And then he'd caught himself, hadn't he? Caught himself on the way to saying that he wished he'd been with her walking through the city that morning, and in the blink of an eye, it had all come rushing back, that *she* was the one who had pushed him out of the nest, the one who'd filled Dad's bandwidth—Dad, who was all he had left because Mum had chosen Gabe over him, deserted him when he'd been trying so hard to fill the hole in her heart Pete had left! Crashing over him like a wave that *Quinn* knew stuff about Lisbon because she was firmly, eternally, in Dad's fricking camp! God help him, in that split second it had exploded to the surface, all the animosity he'd pushed down, all the hurt and anger.

Oh, the chagrin! To have caught himself flowing towards her—*the enemy!*—flowing towards that place with her that he had sworn off going to with any woman ever again. When she would only hurt him too, reject him as Mum had. As

Louise had, at uni, after he had risked his heart with her, trusted her with his story, poured out all his pain, all his venom over Dad and Quinn's precious little party for two. She'd wrapped him up, loved him, only to cut him loose six months later. Too intense, she'd said. Too messed up!

Too much for Louise. Not enough, not important enough for Mum. He'd made up his mind then: no strings, no pain. Hook-ups only. Easy enough to come by at uni and at the casino. Added bonus—Dad disapproved. Oh, the pure joy of payback, of shoving Dad's nose right in it, watching it wrinkle every time he brought a woman home and led her upstairs. Not as often as Dad made out when he was bending his ear about it. Not a *'constant stream'*. Just more than Dad himself who, as far as he could tell, wasn't getting any action at all!

All of it exploding, hitting the fan in that nanosecond in Lisbon, making him want to lash out at Quinn, sting her. So he'd grabbed a spanner to throw in the works, the question he was ninety-nine percent sure he already knew the answer to, just to watch her squirm. Oh, but she had come back at him with such honesty, talking such sense, that it was he who was left squirming, teetering on the edge. And he couldn't find a foothold, a way out of the mess he'd made, so he'd shut down, closed himself off, hurting her more. Evidence of it in her eyes, all over her beautiful face. But she'd remodelled it into a shield to hold against him all the way home, then split without a backwards glance the second her feet hit the ground.

And now he was wretched to the marrow. Aching. He couldn't hold focus at work, at the blackjack table, anywhere. All he could think about was Quinn: the way she'd made him feel before the ugly stuff had twisted him up. Lighter of heart. Freer of spirit. Like his old self. As if anything was possible. Tenderness. Intimacy. Love…

He flagged a cab and got in, turning his gaze through the window. All the things he'd put at the bottom of his list. At the top was making it in Dad's world, making Dad proud of him, but he had smashed through that barrier years ago, ceased to think about it, because he had found his niche in the business, was happy in it. His heart caught. It was the rest of his life that didn't make sense now. And maybe that was because Dad wasn't here any more to provoke, or maybe it was because of Quinn.

He drilled his fingertips into his temples. If he could turn back time he would, undo the hurt, because maybe she was the enemy in his messed-up head, but in his messed-up heart she was golden, the thrill he couldn't stop feeling, and he wanted to see her, say sorry, fix things. But every time he went to call her, he lost his nerve because fixing things would mean untangling threads that might ignite another bitter fuse inside him, cause another conflagration.

He dropped his hands to his lap. But he had to do something. Three and a half weeks since he'd broken their wheel. The longer he left it, the harder it would be to fix. Like Dad's blasted hotel.

Three and a half weeks...

He felt a tingle. A reasonable enough period, surely, to make another site visit feel appropriate. Sensible, even.

Filipe Alexandre was doing a good job of keeping them well appraised but, even so, this was *his* project. Wanting to cast his own eye over things was completely reasonable, and wanting his interior designer present was also completely reasonable. And he was in Paris next week, anyway, which was even better. He could fly to Lisbon from there, meet Quinn at the building like last time, assuming she could make it, would agree to come…

His stomach dipped. If she did, would she suss that he was taking a leaf out of her book, meeting her there to avoid the awkwardness of flying over together, meeting her for the first time since their last visit, with Filipe between them to temper the air? And if she sussed that, would she see that what he was trying to do was make amends and, if she did see that, would she let him?

CHAPTER SEVEN

'HE EMAILED YOU?' Sadie looked up from putting on her jacket, her expression halfway between cross and curious. 'And what did he have to say for himself? *Sorry*, by any chance?'

Her heart crimped. Maybe she shouldn't have mentioned the email, just that she might need to swap a couple of shifts, but since the older woman was her friend as well as the shelter manager, and since she had mercilessly bent her ear about Will, she could hardly blow her off now just because she was in turmoil and didn't want to talk about it.

'That would have been a nice touch, but no...' She pulled her own jacket on, using the moment to push down the hurt. 'He wants us to go see how things are going with the building.'

'Will there be anything to see yet?'

Her own first thought exactly! Filipe was keeping them up to speed with progress, but it was still early days. Her second thought, which she'd instantly discounted as too needy and pathetic to entertain, was the one that was busy surfacing in Sadie's light green eyes.

'Do you think he could be using the trip as an excuse? As a way to see you?'

She offered up a shrug, not trusting herself to speak.

'Perhaps he's feeling bad…' Sadie was running up her zip now, her expression brightening. 'Maybe he wants to see you face to face so he can apologise.'

Something snapped inside.

'He could apologise face to face here, Sadie! Where we both *happen* to live. He's only had, let me see, three weeks, three and a half days to pick his moment.'

'Not that you're counting…'

She felt her bristles stiffening then collapsing. Sadie was only trying to lighten her up, but she couldn't make herself feel lighter, not even for Sadie.

She swallowed. 'I'm sorry but that isn't helping.'

Sadie nodded slowly. 'I can see that—' little shrug '—sorry.' And then she was letting out one of her deep wise sighs. 'You know, Quinn, maybe things aren't quite what they seem with him. I mean, we see it with our service users all the time, don't we? Behaviours that can make you think one thing about a person, then you find out there's more to it, more to them.'

Her heart caught. 'But the *more* part is what I *thought* I'd found! We were getting on, having fun. I thought we were connecting.' And then he'd flicked the switch, pitched her into blinding darkness. She felt an edge hardening somewhere. 'But clearly, I was wrong. I don't know what's real with him and what isn't—what makes him tick, who he is!'

Sadie's eyebrows slid up. 'You'd like to find out though, wouldn't you?'

Her stomach locked. Would she? Still? In spite of everything?

That light in his eyes… That mad thing he'd done with his hair to make her laugh… The way the corners of his mouth curved up just before he smiled. They way he'd saved her, held her without awkwardness, looking at her as he had that other time, when she was seventeen, concern etched on his face, kindness. All the good in him. Her heart twisted. But he'd stung her too, more than once. How many times before she was a mug? How much, even for Anthony's sake, could she take?

She reconnected with Sadie's gaze. 'I don't know. I keep thinking about Liam, all the effort I put in, the big fat nothing I got out of it.'

Sadie rolled her eyes. 'Liam O'Connor was a waster, transparent from the start.' She turned to her locker, pulling out her street-duty rucksack.

'I told you to watch yourself with him right after I met him that first time. Look past the roses, I said.'

She felt her neck prickling. Sadie had said that. But what made her think Will wasn't a waster too? It wasn't as if she'd met him, taken his measure.

'So now you're saying, what? That I should look past the thorns…'

'I'm just saying don't be too quick to judge him, that's all.' Sadie sighed. 'From what you've said, it seems he's had a lot to contend with in his life.'

Her heart gave a little. Nothing she didn't feel to her bones for him, even now. But still…

'So have I, but I don't ride roughshod over other people!'

Sadie shook her head. 'I'm not saying what he did was right, Quinn, but I think you should give him time.' And then her gaze was softening, reaching in, full of kindness. 'Yourself too.'

Time. In Lisbon. Getting tied up in Will Thacker's capricious knots!

'Well, I don't have much choice as far as that goes, do I?' She yanked her rucksack out of her locker, fighting a sudden urge to slam the door shut. 'This isn't a quick makeover job we're trying to pull off, so Will and I are going to have lots more *lovely* time together!'

'Come on, Quinn.' Sadie's tone was cajoling now. 'He saved you from that hole in the floor, tried to take the blame for the whole thing, then went back for your stuff. There's a good guy in there somewhere.' Her gaze lit. 'Plus you like him. Tingles were mentioned. Goosebumps…'

Should have kept her mouth shut!

She shouldered her pack. 'I did like him, yes. Now I just feel like an idiot!'

'Maybe he feels like one too…'

'Oh, I doubt that!'

Nothing remotely sheepish about the way Will had sat on his phone talking business all the way to the airport! In the lounge as well: call after call. Oh, and on the plane he'd put his seat back and closed his eyes, taking a moment out of his busy schedule to excuse himself, blaming the lunchtime beer. By the time they'd landed she couldn't even bring herself to look at him. She'd forced herself to say goodbye at the barriers because she couldn't allow herself to be as rude as he was, and then she'd taken off. Maybe he had felt like an idiot then, but since she hadn't looked back to see, it was open to speculation.

'Come on, let's do the rounds.' Sadie was pulling the door open, ushering her through. 'A couple of hours in the London cold will soon have you longing for Lisbon, even if Will Thacker is part of the package!'

* * *

Sadie was right. Checking in with the rough sleepers had definitely given her a bit of perspective on everything. Next to theirs, her problems were beyond trivial.

She sprung the microwave door and took out her cup, going over to the window. Quiet street. Lamplit. Neighbour's cat doing its own nocturnal rounds. She was lucky. Nice roof over her head, not even a mortgage because of Dad's life insurance. A career she loved. Friends. And Sadie, who'd been her tutor at college and was now a cherished friend-cum-auntie figure. Older. *Wiser!*

She sipped her cocoa. She could line up her blessings no trouble, but there was still the enigma of Will. What was *with* him? Why had he suddenly turned on her like that? If only she could see inside his head. Reaching out to her all those years ago, then changing, as Anthony said, after he went to university, growing more and more taciturn. Coming home less and less, keeping himself to the edges of things when he did.

For years now, he had been like a ghost passing through her orbit, only ever appearing in snatches. Car shows when Anthony was putting the Morgan in for the concours, bending over the engine, his deft hands busy with some fiddly thing that Anthony couldn't manage, fixing it but then always leaving straight after. And what about that time at Anthony's lavish Gatsby-themed sixtieth birthday party when she'd gone all out in a glorious silver-fringed flapper dress that had made her feel every inch like Jay Gatsby's Daisy Buchanan? Will had been there at the start, impeccably handsome in his tux. She had caught him looking at her from across the room at one point, thought maybe he would like to dance, but when she had gone to look for him just half an hour later, Marion said that he had left.

For some stupid reason it had stung. Stupid, because it was completely in keeping. Will was a past master at leaving, beating a retreat when he'd had enough, presumably, or got bored. Or when something else appealed more: skiing instead of Christmas; dinner out instead of at home with her and Anthony. Always coming through a door only to stop and turn round again, as if he'd changed his mind. Always changing his mind, throwing himself into fricking reverse!

Reverse, reverse, reverse!

Her heart paused. But what if he couldn't simply reverse, physically remove himself, then what? She felt a tingle, her heart picking up again. What would Will Thacker do if he found himself trapped in a situation he didn't like? For instance, if he found himself forced to travel with someone he had knowingly hurt…infuriated? She bit her lip. Would he perhaps choose to hide in plain sight by making back-to-back business calls? Oh, and when that option ran dry, when it was flight mode time for the phone, would he put his seat back, perhaps, close his eyes, blame it on a single lunchtime beer?

On point, Will!

In character, just different tactics. Curling up. Bowing out. No remorse!

Wait a minute...

She parked her cup on the sill and pulled out her phone, calling up his email.

Hey Quinn. I'm in the Paris office on Wednesday and thought it might be worth coming back via Lisbon to see how things are going. Any chance you could make it for a site visit at eleven o'clock on Thursday morning? I'm jammed otherwise, so it's Thursday or bust for me, at least for a while. I'm keen to meet Filipe—as you are, I'm sure—and to see how the roof's coming on. Totally understand if you're already committed but if you could possibly find a way to make it that would be really, really great! Hope to hear from you soon. Best, Will.

No remorse, but there were lines aplenty to read between, weren't there? Words and phrases jumping out.

Paris office...jammed otherwise...this Thursday or bust...if you could possibly find a way...really, really great!...

She felt her breath stilling. How hadn't she seen it straight away? He was either desperate to check progress on the building or desperate to see her. Her pulse moved up. Desperate to see her but *not* to fly with her. Hence Paris. Hence stealing her own trick, stealing it because he was…

Oh, for goodness' sake!

Was Sadie right after all? Was he feeling bad, feeling like an idiot? Could it be that this trip wasn't about the building at all, but solely about seeing her? She squeezed her eyes shut. Or was she just chasing unicorns again, tilting the mirror to see what she wanted to see like she always did? Everything was a guess with Will. It might really be all about the roof, and meeting Filipe.

Except... He didn't need her there to look at a roof, did he? And if this was only about business then his email wouldn't have been quite so…so… breathless. She slipped her phone back. No. Will wanted her there, no question, and, bruised as she was, it was a stretch to imagine that all he wanted to do was sting her again, in which case was he, in fact, planning to apologise?

Her heart bumped. And if he did, then what? Did she cave, or stick, let herself like him again so that she could move forward with Anthony's agenda? Or would it be better to keep him at arm's length no matter what, let time tell? She bit her lips together. *Great!* So it was back to

Sadie, and giving herself time to look past the thorns, giving Will time to do whatever it was he had in mind.

She folded her arms. *Fine!* She would give him time, go to Lisbon, but she was keeping her wits about her this time. No letting his smile blind her if she found herself in its bright beam. No letting his gaze soften her stupid. And she definitely wasn't flying back with him. *No, no, no!* She would stay the weekend, fly back on Sunday. Hadn't she been playing around with an idea that the hotel rooms should reflect the city itself? She could use the weekend to explore, start gathering inspiration, soak up some lovely Lisbon sunshine while she was at it.

She felt a smile coming. Yes. That would do very nicely. It was the perfect plan.

CHAPTER EIGHT

FILIPE'S GAZE SHIFTED past him. 'Is this Quinn, coming now?'

His stomach lurched, or maybe it was his heart. Hard to separate the two when his insides were bunched together like this, twisting as one. Maybe he shouldn't have positioned himself with his back to the street end, but having sight of the corner would have been too distracting. It had seemed better to face Filipe, to at least give the man the impression he was fully attentive, which he wasn't. Not by a long mile. Because of Quinn. Because, forty minutes after take-off, his brilliant plan to come straight from Paris to avoid awkwardness had started to seem a lot less brilliant and a lot more like the act of a coward, and the thought of seeing that in her eyes, along with all the other damage he'd caused, was churning him up inside. But he'd made his bed now so…

He took a breath and turned, felt his heart rising against a cold plunging tide. Quinn indeed, coming up the street as before, except this time she was in plimsolls, loose pants and a soft-looking shirt, all cream. Her tote was orange, of course.

He swallowed his heart back down. 'Yes, that's her.'

'She's going to need a jacket on inside.' Filipe glanced over, gesturing to his own clothes but meaning Quinn's—that they would get dirty.

'Yes, probably a good idea.' He smiled, trying to seem casual, to seem as if he wasn't frantically trying to read her mood. Impossible, given that she was focusing on the pavement ten paces in front of her. Was that deliberate, so she didn't have to look at him, or was she simply watching for loose cobbles, of which there were many. Was she going to give him the cold shoulder? Fair enough if she did, but still, the thought of it…

Breathe, Will.

She was here, wasn't she? She'd come. Although what did that really count for since she was bound to the project, the same as he was? Her email had been efficient but not unfriendly. In fact, borderline cheery. He had felt a wave of euphoria reading it, anyway. That was the thing to hold onto and the fact that she was looking up now, smiling on approach. At Filipe.

'Filipe…' She stretched out her hand for the project manager to shake. 'Lovely to meet you.'

'Nice to meet you too, Quinn.' Filipe was twinkling, obviously smitten. 'I was just saying to

Will that you'll need a jacket on in there to protect your clothes from the dust.'

Her gaze stayed on Filipe, along with her smile. 'One of those fetching hi-vis ones, I hope!'

Filipe chuckled. 'They're all the rage inside, along with the hats. Very "in".'

She laughed back. 'Well, I'm nothing if not an ardent follower of fashion, so please, do your worst.'

His chest went tight. She wasn't looking at him, smiling at *him*. Was she punishing him? If so, it was working. He could feel cracks opening inside, pain poking its fingers in. He scanned her face, looking for signs of cruel intent. A suggestion of tension along her jaw. Her smile a touch too wide, not quite reaching her eyes…

His heart pulsed. *Idiot!* She probably would like to punish him, but that wasn't what she was doing at this moment. Likely she was struggling to meet his eye because of the pain he'd caused her. Easy to be casually cheery in an email. Hadn't he pitched his own that way? But face to face was a different story. Doubtless, she was waiting for him to make the first move, which was entirely right since he was the one who'd broken them in the first place.

Come on, Will.

He collected himself and smiled over. 'How was your flight, Quinn?'

She stiffened for a beat, and then she was turning, regarding him with a level gaze. 'It was okay, thanks…'

He felt his ribs tightening as something shifted behind her eyes. For a piece of a second it stilled and then there was movement, a smile ghosting over her lips.

'Somewhat better than the last one.'

His stomach clenched. Talking above Filipe's head. He searched her gaze. Did she expect him to respond? Did he have a choice? Because not responding might seem like a rebuff and he couldn't do that to her again, not when the whole point of this trip was to make things right.

He drew a breath. 'Yeah, that wasn't such a great flight.'

Her gaze narrowed with interest. Or maybe it was surprise. Either way, it seemed as if she was expecting more.

He licked his lips to buy a second. 'It was a bit…bumpy.'

'Bumpy?' Filipe handed them hard hats. 'Did you hit some turbulence?'

Quinn flashed Filipe a smile. 'Yes, we did.' And then her gaze was on his again, bolder now, challenging. 'One moment we were cruising along just fine, then the next: wham!' She put her hat on, reaching round to adjust the band, eyes still trained on his. 'I'd be interested to know the science behind that.'

Filipe shifted stance. 'Fast-moving air currents.'

He ground his jaw. Could Filipe not read the situation, see that this would be a good time for him to go and measure something?

'Pretty scary, huh?' The man was grimacing now, looking at each of them in turn.

He mirrored the grimace to be polite, then rammed his own hat on. He had felt scared, sitting at that table with Quinn, before the mayhem took him over, and he would have to try to explain himself to her, but there weren't enough meteorological metaphors in the world to cover the necessary bases, none that Filipe wouldn't pick up and run with anyway. If only he could bail out of the conversation somehow, but if he did Quinn might feel as if he was shutting her down so, not an option. All he could do was keep going…

He secured his own hat, fastening his eyes on hers to block Filipe out. 'Re the science, it could have just been a…a rogue current. Or a…a spontaneous electrical storm close by that caused that sudden fatal drop. Chaos in the cockpit, instruments spinning, complete loss of control—'

'Don't listen to him, Quinn.'

For the love of God!

Filipe was shaking his head, grinning. 'Will's teasing you. Pilots never lose control. And the planes are built to withstand electrical storms. It can be frightening sometimes but you're always safe.'

Quinn's gaze slid to Filipe. 'Well, that's reassuring.' And then she was turning back, the hint of a twitch playing at the corner of her lovely mouth. 'As for you, teasing me like that…'

He felt his heart pause and then suddenly it was off again, beating hard happy beats, because her eyes were filling with light that looked like laughter, laughing at Filipe and the snafu they'd got themselves into. And it didn't mean he was off the hook, but the ice was broken, lying in pieces all around, and it was such a weight off that he could barely believe he was standing on the pavement not floating above it.

Her gaze held his for one more heartening second and then she was turning to Filipe. 'Shall we go inside now? I'm dying to see what's going on in there. Also, I'm feeling quite excited about this lovely jacket you promised me…'

'I know I've said it already, but I'm amazed at what you've achieved in three weeks, Filipe.' Will was stopping yet again, casting his eyes around, and then he looked over. 'Don't you think?'

She felt her heart squeezing. Ever since they'd come inside he'd been conferring at every opportunity, catching her eye, holding onto her gaze as if he was trying to keep the plates spinning, as if he was scared that if he didn't she would go cold on him.

As if! Not after he'd replied, *in metaphor*, to

her gibe about the flight, the gibe she couldn't keep in because the bad Quinn inside her wanted a little payback. And then Filipe had chimed in, turning the whole thing into a comedy, and she had tried not to show Will that she was laughing inside because the root cause of it—the hurt he'd caused her last time—wasn't remotely funny, but he'd been looking at her so earnestly, his face such a picture—and so damn handsome—that she couldn't keep it from him, not for the world. And maybe that wasn't keeping her wits about her, but that didn't seem important now. What was important was that Will hadn't tried to dodge her bullet, which meant Sadie was right. He was feeling bad about last time, wanted to make amends, and that changed everything…

'Absolutely.' She shot him a smile. 'It's like a different building.' And then, because his steady gaze was stirring warmth in her cheeks, she turned to let her eyes make one last sweep.

So very different, as she'd known it would be, as she'd told him it would be. Gone was the stale damp smell. Gone were the cold and the gloom. Now sunlight was streaming in through the opened-up windows, illuminating a haze of dust—because the place was teeming with builders: banging and scraping; hammering and drilling; shouting and laughing; clomping up and down the stairs and across the floors in their heavy boots.

'Well, we put a big team on it as you asked,

Will.' Filipe was standing with his hand on the newel post, waiting for them, and then he was leading the way back downstairs, raising his voice above the din as he went. 'The floors are all sound now, so we can really crack on. And in a couple of weeks the roof will be fully watertight, not that we're likely to get much rain.'

Will's eyes glanced into hers as he stood back for her to go first, his voice dipping low. 'Good news about the floors.'

She felt the warm tug of before, the bond that was still there somehow, in spite of everything. She couldn't hold in a smile.

'Indeed.'

And then they were descending and she was tuning in to the scuff of his following feet, imagining his lovely face and the smooth curve of his shoulders in his green-and-white-striped shirt. And she could feel her stomach tensing because very soon they were going to be alone and she was dreading it, but at the same time she couldn't wait. And then it was the last step and she was following Filipe along the wide hallway, through the open door, and out into the bright hot glare of the midday sun.

'Any final questions?' Filipe gestured to their hats, indicating that they could remove them.

Will peeled his off, handing it over. 'I guess my only question concerns timeframe.' He raked at his hair, then glanced over. 'Specifically, how long before Quinn can get involved?'

Still in a tearing hurry, which meant Anthony couldn't have revealed all her creative, time-consuming ideas to Will in his letter after all. It was a relief, knowing for sure, except that now, on top of everything else they needed to talk about, she was going to have to raise it, and that could be tricky.

'At least a month…' Filipe's eyes found hers. 'Although if you could take a look at the plans for the proposed bar and lounge area soon that would be useful. I'll need your final decisions on layout so we can get the plumbing and wiring in the right place.'

'No problem.' She slipped off the hi-vis, handing it back with her hat. 'I've got some ideas sketched out already.' No need to say that they were only half baked because her mind had been elsewhere for the past month. 'I'll work on them some more when I get back and send you something as soon as I can.'

'Great!' He put out his hand. 'Nice to meet you, Quinn.'

'Likewise. Thanks for your time today.'

Then it was Will's turn to do the hand shaking and the pleasantries.

And then it was all done, and Filipe was going back inside and, finally, they were alone.

CHAPTER NINE

He pulled in a breath. He was all scudding pulse and wrenching gut, but he wasn't holding this in for another second, not when she had let him back inside her gaze before they'd even set foot in the building, carried on engaging with him as they went around, talking and smiling, not just for show, for Filipe's benefit, but for real. No frost. No daggers. He owed her this from the depths of his heart.

'I'm sorry about last time, Quinn. So, so sorry…'

Her eyes welled slightly. 'I know.' And then she was blinking, smiling a bit. 'You wouldn't have tried to explain yourself in meteorological terms if you weren't.'

'I couldn't not try.' He felt his heart catching. 'I wanted to show you I was ready to talk about it, explain…'

She gave a soft nod. 'So, what happened, Will?'

And now here it was, all the hurt surfacing in her eyes, all the pain and confusion he'd caused. His heart clenched. She deserved a five-star explanation, toffee sauce, sprinkles and a flake, but now that the moment was here, what could he say?

That he'd caught himself liking her, *more* than liking her, and it had thrown him for a loop—triggered some hateful gremlin inside, whispering to him, reminding him that she was the enemy, the one who'd come between him and Dad, stirring him up so much that he'd derailed them on purpose; that once he'd done that he couldn't find a way back, so he'd shut down, even though it hurt to do it—and hurt her as well?

He ran his eyes over her face. Even if she took it on the chin that she'd been the secret object of his animosity for over a decade she would want to know why, and then what would he say? Because the answer was a twisted vine with deep tangled roots, roots that reached into the darkness, and if he couldn't even make himself go there, how could he go there with her? But he had to say something, something true that also tied in with the meteorological metaphors.

He drew in a breath. 'I had a bit of a meltdown.'

Her lips pursed. 'Yes.'

Good going, Will!

Telling her something she knew already. He felt his pores prickling. Maybe moving would help.

He motioned to the street end. 'Can we walk and talk, find some shade?'

She hesitated then nodded. 'Okay.' And then

she was diving into her bag, coming up with sunglasses. 'Do you mind if I wear these?'

'Why would I mind?'

She made a sombre shuttering motion with her hand. 'Hides the eyes. Windows to the soul and all that.'

He turned to walk, feeling an unexpected smile rising. 'Listen, I don't need to see your eyes to know your soul is good. It's mine we should worry about.'

'We'll see.' He felt her shoulder nudging his arm, a little playful, but then her tone was downshifting, serious again. 'So, about this meltdown?'

His stomach roiled. No way round it. The only option was to come clean, put his heart on the block, at least partially, because how could he explain it otherwise? Just a layer or two, peeled back carefully, and then maybe, somehow, the rest would come to him…

He glanced over. 'I think it happened because I didn't expect to like Lisbon so much.' He swallowed hard. 'Or you, Quinn.'

'What?' She stopped dead, pushing up her sunglasses, the windows of her soul displaying an array of indecipherable comings and goings. 'What did you say?'

Was she really making him repeat it? Hard enough saying it the first time. But he was in the thick of it now. No choice.

He inhaled. 'I said that I didn't expect to like it so much here or…'

'Yes…?'

His heart pulsed. *This* was the part she most wanted to hear—that he liked her! He felt his eyes staring into hers, his breath trying to leave. How could it mean anything when, aside from that one time, he had never given her the time of day, never done anything worthy of her attention or favour? Yet here she was, waiting for him to say it, anticipation burning in her gaze as if it mattered, as if *he* mattered, counted somehow, to her.

Beyond feeling!

He felt the air softening, a smile coming. 'Or… to like *you*, Quinn. But I do like you. Very much.'

Her gaze stilled, then it was filling with a glow, lighting up with a smile that caught him in the throat. 'I like you too.' But then in the next moment the glow was fading, and she was frowning, puzzling. 'But you didn't expect to like me?' She looked down for second, blinking, then her eyes came back, wide, wounded. 'Why? Can you unpack that, and the whole meltdown thing as well, because I don't understand…'

His heart seized. Of course she didn't because, aside from that slip at Dad's funeral, he'd always tried to keep his feelings hidden. Must have done a better job of it than he'd thought too, because she seemed not to have the slightest inkling. A good thing for her sake, but a problem for him, because being honest, which he wanted to be, without potentially hurting her all over again, which he definitely didn't want to do, didn't leave him much rope. And yes, thinking about all of this beforehand would have been a good plan, but he hadn't wanted to sound rehearsed, like he was trying to save his own skin, instead of whatever this was sounding like.

Think, Will!

And then suddenly it was opening up. A path through the tangle. Somewhat treacherous, but a path at least.

He drew in a breath, nodded into her gaze. 'Yes, I can. I mean, I'll try to.' Anything to fix this, to bring her smile back. He swallowed to buy a moment, then looked into her eyes. 'You know how Dad and I didn't see eye to eye on this project?'

Small nod. 'Yes.'

'Well, maybe you also know...' Because who knew what Dad had told her? 'Or maybe you don't, but that's a ball with a very long chain.'

Curiosity flared in her eyes, but he wasn't going to elaborate, dig down into that particular crypt. This was only about context.

'Where I'm going with this is that I might have let the project become a bit of a totem for all that stuff with Dad, used it as a legit way to harangue him—I say *legit* because the hotel is, without a shadow of a doubt, a terrible investment.' He felt his chest tightening, his voice tightening with it. 'You probably got that I couldn't fricking well believe the will! Red mist central! Forcing me to take it on, *knowing* I was dead against it. Way to rub—no—*grind* my nose right in it!'

Breathe, Will.

'My total bad, of course, for going in there expecting a smooth ride: something for Mum, a chunk to charity, the rest to me. I was going to put the place straight back on the market, but instead—'

'You were lumbered.'

'Understatement alert!'

Her eyes flickered, registering the reference, and then her gaze cleared. 'So you set your face against it.'

'It was already set. The will just set it harder.'

'And, by association, I was included?'

His gut tensed. He could see the hurt in her eyes, but he couldn't bail now. He'd led her here after all. If he didn't admit to some resentment, then this explanation wasn't going to fly, but he needed to tread softly.

He nodded. 'Honestly—yes, but I knew it was wrong to feel that way. You didn't write the will. None of this is your fault. You're tied, like me.'

She let out a sigh. 'Okay.'

'When we came out last month, I was resigned to just getting on with it since I couldn't change it, but I wasn't feeling it…' An image flew in, making a smile tug: Quinn, raking at the wall with her pen, scattering debris. 'Not until you took me in hand, tried to open my eyes up—'

She puffed her cheeks out. 'Your eyes were more open than mine! You were the one who saw the hole in the floor.'

'It's not the only thing I saw…' He felt the guilt shifting again. 'After what happened, I knew I had to take my share, show you I was stepping up.'

A smile touched her lips. 'It wasn't lost on me. You were on fire with Julia after.'

'And I felt better for it, for involving myself. And then we went for lunch, and it was so warm, and pleasant. And I was looking at the view…' *and you* '…thinking how wonderful everything looked…' *especially you* '…and you were telling me bits of history, telling me about your walk, and I found myself thinking how nice it would have been to be with you…'

'But then…?'

His insides coiled. The trickiest part—building a bridge between the warm fuzzy stuff and what happened next. The truth with a small change of emphasis…

He swallowed hard. 'Okay, just bear with me

here. You know how sometimes when you're falling asleep you can suddenly jolt awake because you've fallen off a kerb or something?'

Her eyebrows went up. 'You fell off a kerb?'

'Yes, sort of…' This had sounded so much more plausible in his head. Would she get it, understand at all? He inhaled, tightening his gaze on hers. 'In that moment, it's as if I suddenly caught myself in the act, liking Lisbon, getting sucked in. I remembered it was Dad's dream, not mine—something he thrust upon me, something I was angry about, tied to because of him, and because of that I shouldn't be letting myself enjoy anything about it.'

Her mouth tightened. 'So then you thought, what…?' Hurt was surfacing in her eyes, glistening. 'That since you couldn't enjoy it, you might as well dump on me, stop me enjoying it too?'

'No!' His heart seized. 'It wasn't like that! It was nothing against you! It was all me—my mess…total internal combustion. Meltdown! And I couldn't level myself out afterwards, so I shut down. And I know that hurt you, and I'm sorry because you didn't deserve it.'

She looked away. 'No, I didn't.'

His heart sank. After all that, turning her head away, not forgiving him. What could he do, say, to turn this around?

You could play your last card...

He paused to breathe, pushed his hands through his hair. 'I wanted to call you, Quinn. To say sorry. I got my phone out a million times to do it, but after the way you strode off at the airport, I couldn't get up the nerve.' He swallowed hard. 'So, I thought if I engineered a trip…'

Her gaze swung back, interested now. 'Engineered?'

'Yes.' He could feel the tips of his ears starting to blaze but if this was what it took… 'I wanted to see you. Fix things. I thought I'd stand a better chance if I made it seem like it was business.'

She inclined her head. 'I did wonder.'

His pulse quickened. Her gaze was brightening, opening by a few heartening degrees.

He ventured a half-smile. 'But you said yes, anyway.'

Her eyes flashed. 'I was curious, okay? I didn't like the way we left things and I figured, since you seemed desperate to tack this trip onto the end of your Paris trip, that it was possible you were feeling the same.' She dipped her chin at him. 'Unless not flying—*avec moi*—from London was pure coincidence?'

Rumbled! But what better feeling than when it was coupled with seeing amusement growing in those gorgeous gold-brown eyes?

'Not a coincidence, no.' He couldn't hold in a smile. 'I did wonder if you'd spot it.'

Her eyes flared. 'What—the pupil becoming the master?' And then, joy of joys, she was laughing, that same infectious chuckle she'd let loose on him in the boardroom that day. 'Only completely totally!' And then she was shaking her head. 'Seriously, though, initial awkwardness aside, it would have been so much easier talking in the airport lounge using plain speech, instead of outside the hotel in code with Filipe chiming in every two seconds. He must have thought we were both mad as hatters!'

Warm eyes. Warm smile. Was he forgiven? He couldn't push her to say it. The main thing was they were through it, *somehow*, sweltering on this pavement but smiling at each other, twinkling.

He offered up a shrug. 'I'm not saying every idea I have is a good one.'

'Can I quote you on that, as I see fit?'

Adorable mischief in her eyes. How could he possibly say no?

He opened his palms. 'Any time.'

She grinned. 'Good!' And then she was turning to look along the street, still smiling. 'So, now that we've sorted all that out, how about we find ourselves some shade and a couple of cold ones?'

CHAPTER TEN

'THIS IS PERFECT!' Will was smiling round at the pretty square and then his eyes met hers, seeming to light on the small doubt she could feel nagging. 'Don't worry, I'm not going to decide suddenly that I shouldn't be letting myself think that. No more kerbs, Quinn.' He shook his head. 'Been there, done that, not going back.'

Conviction in his eyes. In his voice.

She felt something giving inside, a hot ache filling her throat. Yes, he had hurt her the last time they were here, but now he seemed so aware, so tuned in to her, just as he had all those years ago, standing in her doorway, the same warmth and kindness shining through his gaze now as then. She had let him pass her by back then, but not this time—*no way!*—because just twenty minutes ago he'd looked into her eyes and told her he liked her and, in spite of all the messy explaining that followed, that was a huge step forward, not only because it had touched her stupid, needy heart but because it was going to make carrying out Anthony's mission easier…

She let her eyes loose on his face. Smooth arching brows, straight nose. That adorable upturn at the corners of his mouth. And those eyes, royal blue in this light, windows to a tortured soul. She could feel her heart flowing out, wanting to soothe that soul, because he was under her skin now—*somehow*—must have slipped under when she wasn't looking. Maybe when he'd been pulling her back from the brink that day, or when he'd been messing up his hair to make her laugh. Or maybe it was the subtle but completely obvious desperation in his email that had broken her open, or his gallant stab at explaining himself in front of Filipe.

Whatever!

He was inside her now, running through her veins, beating inside her heart.

Sadie was right! She wanted to know Will—likes, dislikes…all about him. This wasn't only Anthony's mission now, but hers too. She wanted to draw Will close, dig into his shadows, help him find his light—which he might discern any second if she didn't stop staring at him like this and reply to what he had said like a normal, non-misty-eyed person!

She smiled. 'I'm glad because it doesn't get much better than this: hot sun, cold beer…' she glanced up at the riot of violet blossoms above them '…incredible jacarandas!'

He tipped his glass towards her, his gaze soft, his smile fond. 'Incredible company.'

Oh, no! No, no, no! One thing to be feeling him inside her, noticing *him*: the perfect fit of his shirt, the way the breeze was lifting his hair, wafting the light fresh smell of his cologne about, quite another for him to be noticing her. *Flirting!*

Not that she didn't like the idea of it because, heaven knew, she did—Will was super gorgeous! But this wasn't just some cute guy making eyes at her, shooting tingles up her spine. This was Anthony's son! She had to work with him, launch a hotel with him. And all that feeling-him-under-her-skin business aside, he was patently a bit of a mess—with regard to Anthony especially—signs and tells the whole time he was talking, things she couldn't ask him about because she didn't know him well enough yet. And maybe he was right, maybe he wouldn't melt down again over liking Lisbon, or her—*hopefully not her*—but that didn't mean he wouldn't combust over something else, and that something might very well be her ideas for the hotel, their impact on his precious timeframe.

So, however lovely it was to be feeling this sweet electricity shuttling back and forth between them, however tempting it was to flirt back, she mustn't. There were bumps ahead, a million possible hurts waiting for her if she wasn't careful.

She needed to nip it in the bud right now. Tactfully, of course.

She raised her eyebrows at him. 'Oh, stop it! You're just sucking up now, trying to get on my good side.'

'Of course I am.' He smiled a lopsided smile. 'I've been on your other side, and I didn't like it much.'

Her heart squeezed. Damn him and his silver tongue! On the other hand, hadn't he just handed her an opportunity to show him where she stood?

She smiled. 'Well, you're on the right side now: we're friends again! In fact, I think we should drink to it.' She raised her glass towards him, trying to keep her voice casual. 'Friends?'

Something moved behind his gaze, and then he was leaning forwards, touching his glass to hers. 'Friends.' For an eternal, heart-thudding, tingle-inducing second his eyes held hers and then he was setting his glass back down, scanning the square. 'So where are we, exactly?'

On safer ground, thank goodness! She gulped down a mouthful of beer to chase the Will-induced dryness from her mouth then parked her glass. 'I don't know exactly, but the old building behind you seems to be called Carmo Convent, and the kiosk where we got the beers is called Carmo Kiosk, so I'm guessing…Carmo Square?'

He broke a smile. 'Detective Quinn!' And then

his smile was fading. 'Dad would have known, wouldn't he?'

Her heart missed. Was Will actually starting a conversation about his father? To what end? His gaze was almost wistful, definitely tentative. One thing for sure, if she didn't seize the moment, it might slip away.

She nodded. 'Yes, undoubtedly…'

Anthony, who had loved Lisbon openly but had struggled to show real love to this smart, kind, messed-up guy sitting opposite. She felt hot tears welling and looked away to hide it, running her eyes over the graceful arched structure in the middle of the square. Maybe it had been a fountain. No sign of water now, though. Just a group of lively teenagers sitting chatting on the shallow steps around its base. Did they have fathers who loved them, who showed it openly, like Dad had with her?

Don't!

She inhaled to reset, then turned back to Will, drawing up the good stuff with a smile. 'Your dad would have known what that structure over there was, and he'd have known the history of the convent too.'

'You loved him, didn't you?'

Soft blue gaze. Intent.

She felt tears prickling again. 'Yes, I did…' She wanted to add *in spite of everything*, but maybe there were enough eggshells under her feet already. 'I mean, he took me in, gave me a home.'

He nodded slightly, and then he was picking up his drink, settling back in his chair. 'Our dads were at uni together, right?'

She felt a little jolt of surprise. But of course he would know this, must know about her mum too, her whole history. All the things they'd never talked about, and now here they were, getting into it, which was weird but also nice.

She let a smile rise. 'Yeah. They shared a flat for a couple of years. Different degrees though. My dad did History and Politics.'

'And then he went into the Civil Service?' Will's eyes took quick measure then lit with a smile. 'Don't look so surprised. Dad filled me in before you—' And then his expression was changing, clouding. He leaned in again, setting his beer down. 'I'm sorry about your dad, Quinn. It must have been so hard for you, not having anyone…'

Stirring her pain, making it flow. No relatives on Mum's side because Mum had been orphaned as a child, had come to Britain from Nigeria to study architecture. No relatives on Dad's side either because he was an only child born to older parents—Grandad and Grandma—who had both died before she was twelve. All those years, just the two of them, because Dad wouldn't date anyone, no matter how much she'd nagged him. He'd used to say he had his hands full enough with her and that, in any case, Mum was the only one for him. Then, at fifty-one, he'd discovered the lump at the side of his neck…

'Hey…' She felt Will's hand sliding over hers, squeezing gently. 'I'm sorry. I was just… I didn't mean to upset you.'

She blinked, found her eyes were wet. 'You didn't.' She wiped her face with her free hand, smiling to reassure him because he looked so concerned. 'Kindness just stirs up the sediment, that's all. Brings things back.'

He nodded. Deep light in his gaze. Understanding.

But of course he understood. He'd lost his brother, hadn't he? Judy by default. And Anthony… It was what she had thought he was lining up to talk about—Anthony, and the grief they shared—but he seemed to have put them on a different path. Not that it mattered. Any path with Will was a good one.

Incredible that they were sitting here talking like this, after years of only existing on each other's periphery, when only a single piece of the past could be said to properly belong to them. A moment in time. Her stomach clenched. A moment she had let die, possibly to their cost. And now they were skating close to it with this talk of

Dad's passing, weren't they? She bit the edge of her lip. If she took him back to that precious moment in her doorway, opened up about it, thanked him for his kindness, then maybe he would open up in return, keep this sweet momentum going.

She blinked herself back into his gaze. 'To be honest, I don't mind at all that you brought it up because I don't have anyone to talk to about that time.' She let a beat pass. 'Not anyone who was actually there, I mean…'

Movement in his eyes. Recognition. He knew what she was talking about.

She turned her hand over inside his, squeezing so he'd feel how much it had meant. 'You were very kind to me, Will. Sweet.' He was blinking, making a burn start in her throat, behind her eyes, but she wasn't stopping. He needed to know this. 'I've never forgotten the way you reached out to me that day, and I'm sorry I couldn't find it in me to respond, but that's because it *was* hard for me. I was so grateful to Anthony, and to you, but Dad was my everything. Losing him, having to leave my home for yours, feeling everything strange around me was unreal. Even though I knew it was coming down the track, I still couldn't believe how quickly my life changed, that I was truly alone in the world.'

'Quinn—' he was frowning, shaking his head now '—you don't have to be sorry. I didn't take offence, lose sleep over it. I got it.' His hand squeezed hers and then he was taking it back, picking up his glass. 'You forget. At eighteen I was well-acquainted with grief.'

And at thirty-one he was getting edgy, his eyes darting, going past her, as if now that he'd brought up the subject of his teenage grief, he wished he hadn't. Was he worried she was going to press him, push him to talk? She wanted to, because getting to know him was suddenly all she could think about, but not if he wasn't ready, if it was going to cause him pain.

She touched a finger to her own glass, keeping her voice gentle. 'I wasn't forgetting anything, especially that. I just wanted you to know that what you said that day meant the world even though I couldn't show it.'

He put his glass back down, seeming to settle. 'I'm glad then.' He gave a small smile, but in the next moment it was gone. 'I have an apology of my own to make, actually.'

Her pulse picked up. 'Oh?'

'It's why I mentioned Dad—you loving him like you did.' He sucked his cheeks in then blew out a sigh. 'At the funeral I behaved very badly towards you and I'm deeply sorry for that.'

What to say?

But then he was continuing, saving her the trouble.

'I don't know what got into me.' Something checked in his gaze. 'Actually, that's not true. I do know.' He rubbed a hand over his face. 'Dad was there for you, Quinn, so you loved him, and because you loved him you could show your sadness easily. I couldn't do that because…'

She held her breath. Was he about to give her the inside track on what was behind his tricky relationship with Anthony, something she could maybe offset with some small hint from Anthony's letter?

But then he was shrugging, spreading his fingers on the table as if in defeat, sending her hopes plummeting. 'Let's just say that my feelings for Dad were—*are*—less clear cut.' Another shrug and then his eyes came to hers, a little bit hopeless. 'Truth is, I envied you at the funeral because you were feeling all the things we're supposed to feel, and I wasn't. When you put your hand on my arm it felt like, I don't know, you were expecting me to cave, or cry or something, because that's what you were doing, and it just made me feel worse. Lacking…'

So he'd shrugged her off for the guilt and shame of not being able to muster the appropriate feelings. Her heart twisted. If only she could tell him that Anthony had gone to his grave feeling guilty for not being the father he had deserved—that if he had felt 'lacking' at his father's funeral then Anthony was as much to blame for that as he was, if not more.

But how could she tell him that now? Trickling in warm hints from Anthony's letter was one thing, but revealing wholesale that Anthony had shared his guilt and anguish about him with *her* might spark his envy again—that, and everything that went with it—and that could set them back by a mile. Bad enough that her plans for the hotel might do that anyway without adding fuel to the fire.

'I'm not trying to make excuses, Quinn.' His hand touched hers briefly, sending a tingle through her. 'I just wanted to explain, say sorry.'

Always saying sorry when so much of what he was apologising for wasn't his fault.

Enough!

She aimed a smile into his eyes, loading it with all the light she had inside. 'And now you have, and I appreciate it, and I'm okay about it. And now I think we should move on.'

His gaze softened then brightened. 'Literally or figuratively?'

'Both!'

His eyes crinkled. 'What do you have in mind?'

'Seafood! I've heard there's an excellent little place down the hill there. Want to check it out?'

He grinned. 'I think it'd be a crime not to.'

CHAPTER ELEVEN

'SO THIS IS Rua Augusta. And down there...' Quinn was sweeping her arm out like a circus ringmaster, turning her head to follow its line '...is the famous arch!'

He followed her gaze to the end of the street, felt his breath stilling. Pale...towering...magnificent. As if someone had just plonked down a version of the Arc de Triomphe. It drew the eye, then led it all the way through itself to the blue sky and the wispy clouds beyond. Stirring, but utterly present, utterly accessible. Quite something!

He pulled in a breath to dispel an unexpected quiver. Had Dad stood here on these same ornate cobblestones feeling this same surge of emotion? Must have. Because he'd come back to Lisbon time and time again, hadn't he—bought a fricking ruin!

He pushed the thought away and looked at Quinn. 'Impressive!'

Smiling eyes. Warm light. Sunglasses perched on her head, or rather buried in those gorgeous dark curls, curls that were lifting a little in the faint breeze.

He felt the tingle he couldn't stop feeling tingling harder. What was she doing to him? He didn't do relationships, didn't go deeper than a night or two with anyone, but he wanted more of this, of *her*. How could simply being with her, talking to her, feel so liberating, like balm for the soul, when it was also so hard, taking him perilously close to difficult edges, stirring old resentments?

Seeing her eyes welling over Dad in that Carmo place had been tough, twisted the knife inside, but in the next moment she had been welling up looking at him, thanking him for that one time in his miserable life that he'd been decent to her, actually apologising to him for not springing up out of her grief to welcome his effort at comforting her. He had felt surprised she remembered—touched. Although, for some reason, he'd never forgotten it either, so maybe it was just one of those memories that stuck…

'Shall we walk on so you can see it up close?'

She was dropping her shades now, raking the curls back into place—curls he'd felt against his face the day she'd nearly fallen…soft, fragrant, abundant…

He smiled to break the spell. 'Sounds good.'

She smiled back. 'Okay.' And then she was turning, setting off, stepping out like she did.

He fell into step beside her, adjusting his stride to hers, trying not to smile like a total goof. It felt ridiculously good to be walking with her, breathing in little bursts of her perfume. Such a lovely street too—wide, airy, pedestrianised. No high-rises here, no modern city skyline. The pale buildings running either side of them were four storeys high at most. He let his eyes skip along the narrow first floor balconies, then over the tables and parasols of the street cafés they were passing. Glinting glasses. Happy holiday faces. But then his eyes were skipping back to Quinn, because not looking at her every few seconds seemed to be impossible.

Quinn...

Spinning the very air into gold, bringing light to the dark—realisation! To think he'd only ventured into 'Dad territory' with her as a prelude to apologising for his behaviour at the funeral. But by the time he'd finally got back to it after all the detours, it had all become clear in his mind, that what had pushed him over the edge that day was envy. Because he didn't feel as she did, didn't feel as he had at Pete's funeral—insides wringing, heart breaking with every struggling breath—and not feeling like that had put the guilt hex on him, inflamed the rest—anger…respect…love…hate—strands he couldn't twist together into manifest grief, strands that were still tugging him a million different ways.

No wonder he was all over the place. With himself. With Quinn. Flirting with her one moment, holding her hand the next, wanting to soothe her heart. And then it had been *her* hand, *her* palm turning over so that it was scorching his, making his blood rush and his heart pound. Turning over her scorching palm like that after quite pointedly declaring them to be friends. Subtext: *and only friends, so stop flirting with me, Will.* Which was exactly right and probably a very good idea. Except it didn't tally with the warm twinkly vibes she was giving out all the time, vibes he couldn't get enough of. And so here he was again, glancing over, and here she was again, catching him out, flooring him with another of those smiles.

How much easier this would be if he could see her purely as a friend, but something was happening here, something he couldn't control. And he was tied now, couldn't simply bolt as he used to, as he had a million times before. Car shows, when he had gone along expecting it to be just Dad then found she was there too, stealing the show in her trim jeans and smart wellies. Family gatherings when the sight of her with Dad was too much to stomach.

Dad's sixtieth! Looking like some silver angel so he couldn't take his eyes off her. How he'd wanted to go over and spread her wings, touch her, taste her. And then she'd looked up, right into his gaze, catching him *in flagrante* with his tongue hanging out. He couldn't stay after that. The kicker was, he'd felt bad about Dad, worried that he would feel hurt that he'd cut out, but he'd never said a thing. His stomach clenched. He probably didn't even notice.

Oh, and now here he was again, seething about Dad, grating himself raw over what Dad did or didn't notice. If Dad had spent less time noticing what he chose to do with his leisure time and more time noticing that his actual sphere of interest at Thacker was commercial development, not commercial suicide, then he might have thought twice about lumbering him with a crumbling folly, one he couldn't wait to—

'Hey, you!' Quinn was eyeing him through her shades, frowning a little. 'I'll give you a penny for them.'

He felt his muscles loosening, a smile coming. 'Believe me, they're not worth that much.' He aimed a finger at her forehead. 'And definitely not worth wrinkling your brow over.'

'Hmm.' Her lips curved up. 'I'm not convinced but I'll let it lie.'

Just as well. When it came to the millstone, she was firmly in Dad's camp. He was on board, true—*committed*—but being on board didn't make the whole thing a good idea.

And then suddenly she was pushing up her sunglasses, filling his gaze with hers. 'Will, I need to talk to you about something.'

His stomach dipped. Anxiety in her eyes. Disquiet. Was it something about Dad, something that was going to grind his gears? Or was he just grabbing at that because he was self-absorbed? He searched her face. It could be something else—something personal to her. Maybe she needed help with something—advice…support. He felt the flurry inside subsiding. He could do that: be sensitive, supportive.

'Okay.' He smiled, loading his gaze with understanding vibes. 'Hit me.'

'It's about the hotel…'

'Oh.' He felt a sudden, ridiculous urge to laugh. The hotel was safe territory. There was nothing she could say about the hotel that could touch him. Dad had seen to that. He opened his palms. 'What about it?'

Her eyes held his for a long beat and then she drew in a breath of the fortifying variety. 'I know you're keen to get the renovation done quickly so you can get rid of it—'

'Too right!'

Something flinched in her gaze, catching him in the chest.

Too forceful, Will!

He drew in a quick breath, smiling to smooth things over. 'Look, I'm not immune to the charms of Lisbon.' He flicked a glance at the great arch to make the point. 'As I said earlier, I'm fast coming round to it as a place, but the hotel is a non-starter!'

Her brow furrowed. 'Did you and Anthony never talk about it…?'

He felt his heart pause. 'What do you mean?'

'I mean, you do know it wasn't about the money, right?'

He felt his bristles stiffening, a fuse trying to blow somewhere. 'It patently wasn't about the money, Quinn, otherwise he wouldn't have bought the blasted thing, so yes, I did get that! And because I got it, at that point I—not very cordially, I admit—declined to show any further interest. So, to answer your question—no, Dad and I didn't talk about it—which I'm sure you know already, so I don't even know why you're asking me.'

She gave a noncommittal shrug, seemingly unfazed. 'I was just checking, that's all.' And then she was stopping, tipping her head back to look at the huge arch that was now right there, towering above them. 'Do you think when this was built the King, or whoever commissioned it, was thinking about cost?'

He followed her gaze, running his eyes over the expanse of pale stone, the mighty pillars, the intricately carved details around its central clock face. There was a statue on top, a figure with arms outstretched, but it was facing away from them, looking out over the square he could see through the arch now, the one she had told him about last time that was right beside the Tagus.

He drew in a steadying breath. 'Probably not, but this is a monument. Its sole purpose is existing. It isn't an eighteen-bedroom hotel that's never going to earn its keep.'

'What if the hotel *could* be made to earn its keep, though?'

The air pulsed. 'I'm sorry…what?'

Her eyes descended the arch and came back to his. 'It's what I want to talk to you about, but please…' She stepped in close, putting her hand on his forearm. 'Would you let me say everything I have to say before you say anything?'

Not a problem since he was close to speechless anyway.

'Okay.'

She took her hand back, beckoning him to follow her to a shaded area by the plinth, and then she was turning, fastening her eyes on his. 'As you've just so eloquently confirmed, when Anthony bought the building he wasn't thinking about profit. He just loved this city, hated to see so many elegant buildings going to ruin. He thought if he could buy one it would be a fun little project to work on, something different.'

Like a money pit!

'As you also know, he asked me if I'd like to be involved, which I did, obviously. He wasn't all that clear about what the hotel should be other than that he wanted it to be different to the standard Thacker offering.'

Fair enough. Dad had built the business on the back of a model that had barely changed in thirty years after all, but still, maybe because she was suddenly speaking more quickly, he could feel his pulse quickening, a vague unease ebbing up his spine.

'Even though Anthony wasn't bothered about the money, my first thought was the same as yours, that with the cost of the reno and with only eighteen bedrooms the hotel would be a long time coming into profit. My second thought was that if we positioned ourselves at the top end, not only would the numbers look better, but Anthony would get something that wasn't just different but properly exciting too.' She swallowed. 'I'm talking an exclusive Lisbon hotel, Will! Every room unique, luxurious. Bespoke boutique!' And then she was exhaling as if she had been holding her breath the whole time. 'What I'm getting to, trying to tell you, is that your dad really liked that idea, that bespoke boutique is basically *the* plan for the hotel.'

His lungs locked. And she'd been sitting on this all this time! When he'd been upfront, honest from the off, crystal-clear about wanting to get this thing done and dusted! Letting him say as much, smiling at him as he'd said it, staying silent, not even a ripple, a hint.

For crying out loud! Didn't this just take the biscuit? Dad's will—lumbering *him*, hanging the project around *his* neck, but this wasn't actually his gig at all, was it? It was the fricking 'Anthony and Quinn Show' all over again. Country walks, car shows, dinners out. Laughing together, cooking together! Well, they'd cooked up a storm this time, hadn't they? Left him high and dry. Out. Of. The. Loop.

Of all the places to tell him, too. On the street… people going by. He ground his jaw hard, willing the burn behind his eyes to stop, his lungs to draw in air. He couldn't lose it. Not here, not while the hurt was biting this hard. The thing to do was stop. Divide. Conquer. Separate out the threads—the Quinn stuff from the Dad stuff; the Dad stuff from the Mum and Pete stuff. Anger…

pain. Loneliness…pain. Resentment…pain. He could feel the sparks jumping, scorching, but he couldn't let them fly. He'd blown it with Quinn before and he couldn't—*wouldn't*—do it again. Not without counting to ten. Not without giving reason a say in the matter.

He forced himself to look at her. Wide eyes. Primed. Anticipating a reaction. Dreading it. He slowed his breathing, pushing everything down. It couldn't have been easy telling him all that. Tiptoeing into it, double checking how much he knew before starting. That long exhale at the end, as if it had been pressing down on her chest for a while, which it must have been, because—*face it*—if he had been standing in her shoes, would he have wanted to tell *him* that the agreed plan for the hotel was not the quick hatch and despatch job he'd thought it was but something else entirely, something protracted and eye-wateringly expensive? He swallowed. No, he wouldn't. Not before he had to, and especially not after their other ups and downs.

He drew in a deeper breath, felt it clearing his head. Fact was, it wasn't Quinn's fault that she was interested in the hotel, wasn't her fault that she had hatched a plan of her own, and it definitely wasn't her fault that from the second Dad showed him the details he had refused to be interested at all. Truth was, if he was out the loop it was as much his fault as hers.

'Will...?' She was worrying at a fingernail with her teeth, something she seemed to do when she was nervous. 'Are you going to say something?'

Because having seized the moment, forced herself to tell him everything, she wanted a reaction. Something—anything but this nerve-jangling silence. And then—*finally!*—his gaze was reanimating, reconnecting.

'Yes, I am...' He sighed. 'I will... I'm just trying to get my thoughts in order.'

What thoughts, though? He didn't look as if he was about to explode, but he didn't look delighted either. He was being annoyingly cryptic—and cryptic wasn't doing her nerves any good. She could feel her arms folding across her front, anxious prompts rising on her tongue.

'Are you upset? Cross?'

'No!'

Straight back at her. Frowning as if she was mad for thinking it but then, in the next moment, he was rubbing his head, offering up a weary-looking smile.

'Don't get me wrong. I was for a moment but I'm past it now. Now, I'm just trying to assimilate...'

Trying to assimilate something he should have

known already, would have, if he and Anthony had ever talked properly, if Anthony had connected with him like a father should, forced himself past his emotional hangups for his son's sake.

She felt her heart softening. 'I'm sorry I didn't tell you before. I wanted to, but I didn't know how you'd take it, if you'd blow a fuse, or feel hurt, or…'

'All of the above?'

'Exactly!'

Her chest went tight. And it wasn't fair, was it? Never knowing which way the wind was blowing. Always having to walk this tightrope between him and his father. And maybe it would clear the air if she just let it all out, told him.

'Will, you've got to understand: this thing between you and your dad makes it hard for me—hard for me to say certain things, to know how to *be* with you about him, or about anything concerning him, like the hotel. We're coming from such different places, you and I…'

Acknowledgement in his eyes. No need to elaborate. He knew what she was saying.

'I wanted to tell you from the get-go, not only because it was the right thing to do, but also to honour your dad, because it was *our* plan, *his* dream…'

A dream he would never see realised now because the cancer had rubbed him out, the way it had rubbed Dad out. She felt her sinuses tingling. Precious lives cut short. Precious time lost—time that Anthony could have used to make things right with Will, that Will could have used…

She swallowed hard. 'But for that exact same reason I couldn't raise it with you! You're all about getting the hotel done quickly, getting rid of it because Anthony forced it on you, and I can understand that…' She could feel grief and anger thickening in her chest now, hot tears clogging her lashes. 'But you also want to throw it off for the simple fact that it was his dream, because you can't stand it, can you?' Something pulsed behind his eyes that made her own well hotter, wetter. 'I don't know what all your issues were with him, and I'm not asking you to tell me, not if you don't want to, but you need to know how it feels for me, Will! I'm stuck in the middle! I want to do right by him, and I want to do right by you, and I care about both of you, but I can't…' She forced a sob back down. 'I can't even *move* in this straitjacket!'

For a second, his eyes stared into hers and then his face was crumpling and he was moving in, taking hold of her face, wiping her tears with his thumbs. 'Oh, Quinn, please don't cry.' Shaking his head, his gaze blue and full. 'I do get it—all of it.' And then his focus was shifting, turning inwards. 'I'm sorry it's such a mess.'

Her heart pulsed. But would he try to untangle it? For her—for himself. That would be a leap towards the light. She could prompt him, perhaps. A tiny nudge. *Except* that would mean speaking, moving, and she didn't want to do either of those things because his gentle touch was giving her tingles, and his body was so close, and her face was tilted upwards in his hands so she was looking at his lovely mouth, and it wasn't much of a stretch to imagine how things could…

'Sorry…' His focus was back, arrowing in, stealing her breath. 'Are you okay?'

'Yes.' Except for her mouth, which was going dry, and her ears, which were pulsing with fast thick heartbeats because now he seemed to be stuck again, locked in the moment, or maybe it was she who was trapped, or maybe it was time stretching, slowing everything down, which was why it was easy to see his eyes lowering to her mouth, easy to see the slow parting of his lips, the tip of his tongue pausing there, then the slow deep swallow, the up down movement of his Adam's apple.

And then suddenly he was jerking his hands away as if she were white-hot metal, pushing them through his hair.

'Sorry…' He stepped back, his hands making a second, slower, pass and then he was sighing at the ground, talking to the ground. 'You must be sick of hearing that from me by now.' He shook his head. 'I'm certainly sick of saying it.'

Sorry for what, though? For looking at her mouth? For thinking about kissing her? Or maybe she had misread, was just projecting her own heat-of-the-moment confusion onto him.

'It's all right.' She inhaled to steady herself. 'We've both got things to be sorry for.'

'Me more than you.' Another sigh, and then his gaze was lifting by tentative degrees, filling hers again. 'I can see I haven't made it easy for you, and I want to wipe the slate clean, but you're going to have to help me.'

Her heart gave. Asking for help, trying so hard. 'Okay, but how?'

He gave a little shrug. 'Just…talk about Dad… if you want to, I mean. Whenever you want to. Don't skirt round him. Or me, for that matter.' He stepped closer, his gaze deep, and full. 'Promise me, Quinn.'

She felt tears aching again, in her throat, behind her lids. This was all for her, not for himself. Because it was still there, moving behind his eyes, that secret pain he kept over Anthony—pain he was forcing himself over, like a hurdle, for her sake. That he was doing this for her maybe wasn't a startling leap towards the light, but it might unlock a few doors. At the very least, it would make talking about the project easier.

She swallowed the ache back down and smiled. 'Okay. I promise.'

'Great!' His eyes crinkled and then he passed a hand across his forehead as if he was, indeed, wiping the slate clean. 'So, now we need to talk about your plan for the hotel.'

Her heart bounced. 'Talk about, as in…'

Did she dare to even hope that he would run with it?

He raised his eyebrows. 'As in: I've got a few things to say about it, but I'm ready to listen and discuss it.'

She felt her lips curving, a mad urge to fling her arms around his neck, but that was out of the question. Besides, he was talking on.

'The only thing is, we should really be making tracks…' He threw a glance at the clock on the arch. 'I've got to get my bag out of left luggage before we go through. We can talk in the cab.'

Her heart stalled. No, they couldn't!

Oh, God!

How had they managed to spend three hours together without once touching on the return journey—a journey she wasn't actually making?

'Quinn?' He was looking at her, his brow furrowing a little. 'What's up?'

Where to even begin?

She bit her lip. 'I'm sorry, Will…'

'What about?'

She swallowed hard. 'I'm not leaving today. I'm staying the weekend, flying back midday Sunday.'

'But…' His gaze narrowed in confusion and then it was clearing, meeting hers. 'Please tell me you didn't do that because of me, because you didn't want to risk a repeat of last time?'

Her heart pinched. No point denying it. He could surely see it written on her face anyway.

She nodded. 'Sort of…'

Pain in his eyes. Regret.

Nothing she wasn't feeling too in huge, desperate spades.

She licked her lips quickly. 'It wasn't the only reason, though…' Which might soften the blow for him, if not for herself. 'I thought it'd be good to spend some time here exploring the city. I've got this idea, see, to draw inspiration for the individual bedrooms from the city itself. Colours. Textures. That kind of thing. I'm going to look around, see if it could be a viable approach.'

He received this with a slow nod. 'So, where are you staying?'

'The Metropole.'

'Right.' His lips pursed and then he was drawing himself up. 'Well, maybe we could get together in London then, next week, or whenever suits…'

She felt an ache tugging, wretchedness winding through, but if she didn't force herself to seem bright about the prospect then he was only going to feel worse.

'Sure.' She smiled to warm him. 'I'll hopefully have some firm ideas by then—only for discussion, obviously.'

'Obviously…' He smiled a pale confounded smile and then, as if he wasn't sure if it was the right thing to do or not, he stepped in quickly and kissed her on the cheek. 'Have a good one, Quinn!' And then he was turning on his heel, striding away up Rua Augusta, disappearing from sight.

She touched the place he'd kissed, swallowing down tears along with the scream she could feel rising inside.

How could they not catch a fricking break? Why did everything have to keep going wrong?

CHAPTER TWELVE

'UNBELIEVABLE!'

'Sorry, *senhor*?'

Curses! He must have said it out loud. And now the taxi driver was staring at him through the rear-view mirror, obviously thinking he'd missed some fresh instruction.

'It was nothing.' He shook his head at the man, waving his hand to dismiss it. 'I was talking to myself.'

'Ah!'

The driver's expression said it all: *Like a madman!*

Like a mad man who was trying very hard right now *not* to put his mad fist through the window.

He clamped his mouth shut to make sure nothing else slipped out. *Unbelievable!* Why was everything with Quinn one step forward, two steps back? Just when he'd turned himself round, allowed himself to see some merit in her bespoke boutique idea—just when he'd started seeing things from her side, feeling things from her side, fate had drawn a line, dumping him on the wrong side.

He looked out of the window, taking in nothing. Or maybe it was the right side. For him. For her. Because he had just come pretty close to blowing it back there, hadn't he?

His stomach roiled. He had only set out to comfort her. A pure impulse from a pure place because she was crying—because of him, and Dad, and the position they'd put her in—and he couldn't bear it. And she had let him touch her, let him wipe her tears away. No recoiling. No stiffening. Just looking up at him, reaching in with that warm liquid gaze of hers, and then he had got stuck, couldn't shake himself loose, couldn't stop his eyes going to her mouth, imagining how her lips would feel under his, wanting so badly to taste them that he'd almost succumbed…

He shut his eyes. Thank God he hadn't because this was Quinn Radley. In itself a complication too far, never mind that they were working together, hence colleagues, hence off-limits to each other. And even if, for a tantalising second, it had seemed that she was looking at him with longing in her eyes, seemed that maybe she wanted him to kiss her, it was probably just his febrile imagination tripping because she was lovely, because being with her, spending time with her, was reminding his body that it had wanted her ever since the night of Dad's sixtieth.

He rubbed his hands over his face, reconnecting with the view. Just an old thread getting tangled up with the new ones, almost landing him on the wrong side of the line. His heart clenched. But if this was the right side, then why didn't it feel right? Why was his pulse going hard, his fist itching to break something? Why was he feeling devastated that she wasn't here with him, filling his head with her ideas for the hotel? Dad's dream—calling him out for being against it simply because it was that! He swallowed hard. She was right, of course.

He drummed his fingers on his thigh. At least Dad had had a dream, though. What was his? A pang caught him in the gut.

And what the hell was he going to do with himself in London all weekend? Rattle around in the big old house feeling the irksome absence of Dad? Call Mum for a few minutes of awkward catch-up conversation? Hang out with his partnered-up friends, pretending he was cool with being thirty-one and single? Or he could fritter his time away at Aspinalls. Tempting, *not!* And meanwhile Quinn would be here, in the warmth and sunshine, searching for creative inspiration—*alone*. Drinking alone, dining alone, possibly being approached by some random guy. His heart lurched. Not possibly, *probably*, because she was stunning, and far too friendly for her own good…

An airport welcome sign flashed past.

He felt a hot wave rising, pulsing up his spine and then suddenly it stopped.

What the hell was he doing?

Just because he was booked to fly didn't mean he had to! He could cancel, go back, book into the Metropole, spend the weekend with Quinn, searching for colours or whatever, listening to her ideas, thrashing things out. This was business after all. *His* business! Why wouldn't he want to be involved? And it wasn't as if he didn't want to see more of the city…

And if he stayed he could keep an eye on her, because she was bound to go off the main drag, intentionally or otherwise, not thinking of danger. From her own lips—that was what she did all the time! He could keep her safe, protect her from random strangers. And as long as she didn't mind him tagging along then wouldn't it be the perfect opportunity for them to get to know each other better? After everything they'd been through, that couldn't hurt, could only help on the project front, especially now it was sprouting arms and legs.

He felt a smile coming. He wasn't sold yet, but

it was quite the curve ball she'd thrown. A smart take on things. It was giving him a buzz anyway, or maybe the buzz was in collaborating, working with someone who had creative vision. He didn't have much to offer in that department, but he was curious, wanted to learn, and at this very moment his favourite teacher was walking through Lisbon without him. Not a situation he could allow to continue, at least not without giving her an alternative option!

The driver was pulling in now, cutting the engine, turning round. 'Twenty euros, *senhor*.'

He flicked a glance through the window. The taxi queue was heaving, snaking back for miles. If he let this cab go, it would take him ages to get another once he'd retrieved his bag and he didn't have time to waste. He had to get back, find Quinn, see if she was open to the idea of a partner in crime.

He pulled out a hundred, offering it up but keeping hold. 'Could you wait, please? I'm going in, then coming back out.'

The man looked confused. 'You come back, *senhor*?'

'Yes.' He felt his hands moving, trying to illustrate. 'I'm going in to collect a bag, then I want to go back to the city.' He circled his finger so the guy would get it, trying and failing to stop a smile breaking his face apart. 'I'm not leaving Lisbon today.'

CHAPTER THIRTEEN

It was stupid to be feeling this deflated. A solo weekend in Lisbon was exactly what she had planned, after all. Time to explore and gather ideas—ideas which, from the sound of it, Will might actually consider. Lots to feel positive about.

She looked down at her plate, at the untouched tart with its sprinkling of cinnamon on top. It was just difficult to feel positive right now while this big Will-shaped hole was busy expanding inside, a hole that even a custard tart couldn't fill.

Ridiculous!

It wasn't as if they were close…as if she knew him beyond bits and pieces. And heaven knew things hadn't been easy with him, or between them. But she was missing him all the same, aching with missing him. The sight of him. His smile. All his blue depths and warm lights. He was under her skin, she knew that, but seemingly he was much deeper under than she'd thought, so deep that it had been all she could do not to tear up Rua Augusta after him, beg him to stay. If she had, would he be sitting here now or would he have stepped back in surprise, looked at her as if she were mad?

Impossible to say, which was why she had let him go. Because even though it had seemed he was dismayed she wasn't going back to London, she could well have been reading too much into it, projecting her own disappointment into his eyes, seeing what she wanted to see because for a moment back there it had felt as if he was going to kiss her, and the tingling idea of it was taking a long time to clear from her blood, her brain. It was why she was still sitting here in the Praço do Comércio, not a hundred metres from where he had left her an hour ago, trying to fortify herself with coffee and a *pastel de nata*, trying to pull herself back level. But it wasn't working.

And now her phone was pinging. Sadie, no doubt, checking in to see if she had been right about Will, about him engineering this whole trip so he could see her!

She picked it up and her heart slipped sideways. Not Sadie but Will…

Hey, you. How's the exploring going?

She felt a smile rising, breaking, her heart lifting. They didn't do chatty texts, but it was perfect timing. Just the sweet, tingling boost she needed.

She bit down on her lip, texting back.

Not very well. Got waylaid exploring the merits of pastéis de nata at a very nice café in the Praço do Comércio and I'm still here.

Which café?

She felt a frown coming. How could that matter? Still…

Martinho da Arcada.

Ah! Opened 1778. The oldest café in Lisbon!

She laughed out loud, attracting a curious glance from a woman at the next table, but she didn't care. He was filling her well, making her day.

She tapped out a reply, giggling inside.

What??? Since WHEN are you the font of all Lisbon knowledge?

Since I bought a guidebook!

She laughed again, feeling a tease coming.

That'll come in handy in London!

Not remotely! But it's proving useful here…

Her heart bounced. *Here?* But he was at the airport, surely! *Unless...*

She lifted her head slowly, scanning the square to her left, then the arches up ahead, feeling faintly sick, faintly idiotic. And then her heart stopped dead. *There!* Under the great arch. Guidebook in hand. Looking this way and that. And then his eyes found hers, flashing sweet recognition, knocking the air clean out of her lungs. And then he was on his way, coming towards her through the crowd with his nice long stride, walking until he was right there in front of her, smiling, twinkling.

'Hello.'

She felt her eyes staring into his. How to breathe? How to speak when her heart was this full, but then suddenly that brimming heart was jumping her to her feet, and before she knew what she was doing she was flinging her arms around his neck, hugging him for all she was worth.

'For God's sake, Will! What are you doing here?'

He laughed. 'Apart from being strangled, you mean?' And then his arms were wrapping around her in turn, hugging her back. 'Let's just say I couldn't leave. Not when we were on the point of having a very important discussion about the hotel from hell.'

No bile in his voice, though, only lightness. And his arms holding her. No stiffness, no reserve. Just warmth, affection. She breathed him in. Was he really only here because of business, because this hug was feeling more like heaven than business and, wishful imaginings aside, thinking about it again, it had sort of felt that earlier he did want to kiss her…

Oh, hell!

And she had started this hugging. Spontaneously for sure, because it was so good to see him, but if he had been thinking of kissing her before, what must he be thinking now? What signal was she sending out? Aside from the wrong one! Which was the right one, secretly, but that was her business. *Whatever!* In one more second this could turn sticky, and with everything else they had going on—Anthony, and the project, and Will's issues with those things—sticky was the last thing they needed.

She released him quickly, smiling past the annoying blush that was suddenly tingling in her cheeks. 'It was a good call!'

'You think so?' He looked pleased—*relieved*—but then his eyes were clouding. 'You really don't mind me crashing your party? I mean, just say if you do and I'll go.'

After only just getting here! Was he for real? She fired him a look to set him straight.

'There's no party to crash. And there especially won't be if you leave.' She motioned to the table. 'Shall we sit?'

He split a grin. 'Okay.'

She took her own seat, watching him settle. Guidebook, but no bag. No jacket. Had he left them at the airport, or had he booked himself into a hotel? She felt a tingle starting, a vague skittering sensation in her veins. Gorgeous as it was to see him, what was the plan here?

She smiled over, tucking a curl back to seem casual. 'So, now that you're here, how long are you staying?'

His gaze faltered then stilled, clearing into hers. 'That's up to you.'

The tingle skittered into her stomach.

'I don't own Lisbon, Will.'

'No, but you weren't planning to spend your weekend with me either. Just because I took it upon myself to come back doesn't mean you have to fall in.' His lips set. 'I'm not trying to force a situation on you, Quinn, impose myself…'

She felt her heart melting. That he would come back to find her, fully prepared to disappear again if she wanted him to, was beyond adorable.

'You're not, and you wouldn't be.'

'You're sure?'

Still the doubt!

'Of course! Which part of the whole mobbing-you-with-an-unsolicited-hug thing didn't you get?'

He smiled a lopsided smile. 'Now that you put it like that…'

Which maybe she shouldn't have, because now she was thinking about how lovely he'd felt to hug, all smooth cotton and muscular shoulders, and thinking about it was turning her bones to rubber.

She inhaled to reset. 'So, have you booked a place to stay?'

'Yes…' His smile turned sheepish. 'I got a room at the Metropole, actually. I thought staying in the same place made sense, but if you think it's too much…'

What? He was worried that staying at the same hotel, along with the other two hundred or so random people staying there, would bother her! His insecurity was startling but so utterly endearing that she couldn't not smile, couldn't resist teasing him a little bit.

'Well, it is quite stalkery of you, but it's also very convenient! I'll be able to knock you up first thing so we can hit the streets before the crowds get going.'

He smiled, and then his gaze was softening, filling hers. 'You're very nice, do you know that?'

She felt her heart squeezing, heat prickling behind her lids. How was he able to stir her emotions like this, tug her heart out with a word that her English teacher used to strike out for being insipid? There was nothing insipid about it! Nothing insipid about the light in his eyes or the warmth pouring into her chest.

She swallowed to find her voice. 'So are you.'

He baulked. 'Thanks, but I'm not so sure.'

Her heart bumped. Did he not see the good in himself? She so wanted to dig into that, but maybe this wasn't the moment. This moment called for a light touch.

She slid her eyebrows up. 'You're not sure if you're nice or not?'

He inclined his head, faintly wary, faintly bemused. 'I guess.'

'So, why don't you let me decide? Show me your best, nicest side all weekend, and I'll do the same, then at the end we can judge how nice we both are.'

A wry smile lifted his mouth. 'In other words, you want me to suck up to you all weekend?'

She felt a giggle rising. 'If that's what it takes, yes. But remember, it cuts both ways.'

'Hmm…' His eyes darted to her plate, came back twinkling. 'So if I sign up to this pact, do I get to share your custard tart?'

Oh, he was good! Going straight for the jugular.

She looked at the tart, trying to quash another giggle, then met his gaze. 'Asking isn't nice, you know.'

'Oh, I'm sorry.' He pressed a hand to his chest. 'My bad.' And then he was resting his forearms on the table, leaning in, his eyes glinting with mischief. 'You're right, of course. I should totally have waited for you to offer.'

And again! Running his smart rings around her, tickling all of her funny bones at once so that it was getting harder and harder to keep a straight face.

She pursed her lips to stop them from twitching, going for a derisive look. 'You can go off people, you know.'

His eyebrows flashed. 'But not off me, surely, because I'm nice.'

She stared at him hard, trying not to succumb, but then her traitorous lips were curving and his were too, and it was the best feeling in the world to be sitting here laughing together, a custard tart between them and a whole weekend ahead of them, the fun already starting.

CHAPTER FOURTEEN

'SO THIS VIEWPOINT is called...' He licked his lips, concentrating. 'Mira-dour-o de Sã-o Pe-dro de Al-cân-ta-ra!'

Quinn pulled a wincing face. 'Or something along those lines anyway...'

He felt his lips twitching. Always teasing him, just like Pete, making him feel light as air. Carefree.

He feigned chagrin. 'Are you trying to say my Portuguese pronunciation sucks?'

She laughed. 'Not *trying* to...' And then she was smiling into his eyes, doing the placating thing. 'To be fair, I don't know what it should sound like, but I'm fairly sure that *that* isn't it.' And then she was turning, making for the fountain, calling back over her shoulder, 'Ten points for trying though.'

He felt warmth bursting inside. Such a good decision to come back yesterday! Sweet delight on her face when she'd caught sight of him. That unexpected hug! Then it had been the two of them doing battle over the custard tart, until it had struck them that they could simply order more.

Afterwards, they had wandered around the Praço do Comércio, Quinn mulling over the bright yellow walls of the surrounding Pombaline-style buildings as a potential accent colour—*Pombaline-style* and *accent colour* being new phrases in his developing creative lexicon—but then, for some reason, she'd switched to teasing him about his guidebook.

He felt a chuckle rising. Not his fault that random facts were his thing. How could she not have found it fascinating that the square was one hundred and seventy-five metres by one hundred and seventy-five metres, and that before the earthquake of 1775 the site had been home to the royal palace? How could she not have wanted to know that the red suspension bridge they could see to the west was the 25 de Abril Bridge, named for the Portuguese Carnation Revolution of that same date in 1974?

So much fun plying her with facts, seeing her eyes twinkle, feeling it feeding some starved thing inside him, feeding it like a drug. All through dinner too—a candlelit blur on some restaurant terrace overlooking the Tagus—wine and teasing, a few stabs at business chat. Trying—*failing!*—not to lose himself in her eyes, in all her lovely animation.

And now she was playing with a small dog by the fountain, rubbing its head, laughing at its antics. So lovely—too lovely in that sundress, her smooth golden shoulders catching splashes of dappled sunlight, her collarbones dusky with shadow, making his lips want to…

Oh God! Telling himself that this was all about business and keeping her safe was all very well, but there was more going on here, wasn't there? A scary kind of more. The kind of more he hadn't courted—*wanted!*—let himself think about for years. And he didn't want to be thinking about it now, even entertaining it, because this was Quinn—Dad's little pet—the last person in the world he should be thinking about more with.

His stomach seized. But how to switch off these feelings, draw back, when he didn't *want* to dampen anything, when he wanted more? More of her time, her laughter, her loveliness, more of this tingling, glad-to-be-alive feeling. His heart pulsed. And what of her feelings? What would drawing back do except hurt her, make her think he was shutting down on her again? His heart caught. He couldn't do that to her. Not again.

He inhaled, letting his gaze widen. Trees… Paths… People…

Resolution! Nothing for it but to keep the inner crazy well-stoppered and carry on. After all, it wasn't as if anything could happen between them—rules of the workplace and all that. He felt his pulse settling. No… As long as he stayed on the right side of the off-limits line, he was safe, fine to let himself enjoy this for what it was, which, right now, was Quinn coming up, a little breathless, full of smiles.

'Did you see the cute dog?'

He felt his own smile spreading. 'I did.'

'And you weren't tempted to come over, give him a cuddle?'

They seemed to be walking again, heading for the parapet.

'I didn't want to butt in.'

Her eyes narrowed. 'You're not scared of dogs, are you?' And then, quickly, 'Not that there's anything wrong with that… I mean, lots of people are.'

Always that kindness with her, that irresistible warmth of spirit. No wonder he was a barrel of confusion.

He shook his head. 'No, I'm not scared of dogs, although—caveat—if a dog is scary, I reserve the right to be scared.'

She chuckled. 'Well, that little one was soppy. That's my favourite kind: pure-bred soppy!'

'Figures.'

'Are you saying I'm soppy?'

'No, but you're warm.'

She seemed momentarily stunned, and then she

was putting her hands to her cheeks, laughing. 'Especially now, thank you very much. You're making me blush.'

No more than himself, at least on the inside, but twisting it up into a bit of fun would soon cure them.

He put his hands up. 'Sorry, but you know, there *is* this ongoing pressure to be nice!'

She laughed, and then she was drawing in a large breath. 'And on that *nice* convenient note, I'm going to change the subject.'

'To—?'

'The hotel.'

Business—the perfect antidote to whatever this was.

He smiled over. 'What about it?'

'I was just thinking about what you said last night, about the commercial perils of offering choice…'

He felt his business brain waking up. 'Only because consistency is what I know.'

'I get that, but you raised a valid point.' And then she was stopping, turning to face him, her eyes serious. 'If you're a guest looking to pay top whack for a unique room then it *absolutely* follows that you're going to want the room you want, not some disappointing second choice option if that one isn't available.

'And I know I said I've seen it working in London, and that all the rooms should be equally desirable, and that with so few rooms, filling them shouldn't be difficult but see, now I'm wondering if we shouldn't rein back on the bespoke angle a bit.' She gave a little shrug. 'I mean, we could easily go top end with something less avant-garde, less polarising…'

He felt himself staring into her eyes, his heart sinking in his chest. Was she doing this for him? All because he'd raised a point based on his über-narrow experience with the Thacker business model. Talking about compromise for his sake! It was even-handed of her, beyond touching, but he didn't want this. He hadn't come back here to pour cold water on her ideas. Yes, he had questions, but mostly he was enthralled, excited. If she couldn't see that, wasn't getting it, then clearly, he needed to spell it out.

'Quinn, come…'

She blinked. 'Where?'

He felt a flash of impatience and grabbed her arm. 'Just come, okay?' Because there was a gap opening up by the parapet railing which would heal over with other tourists if they didn't claim it quickly, a place where they could talk without getting in anyone's way.

When she was safely installed and looking at him again, he drew a breath. 'Whatever you're thinking, you need to stop, okay? I don't want us to go less avant-garde and I can see from your face that you don't either.'

'But what you said—'

'Is irrelevant.'

'No.' She was shaking her head at him, using a slow, emphatic tone. 'You *have* got a point.'

Were they really here again, arguing the toss, like on the day she'd nearly fallen through the floor? If he didn't nip this in the bud right now, it would run and run.

He pressed his gaze into hers. 'But you've got more points, good ones too. As you just said, we don't have many rooms to fill so there'll always be someone ready to…' He felt a tingle. 'In fact, now I think about it, there's an easy way to circumvent the whole disappointment angle with a booking system that only shows details of the available rooms for the date being searched…'

Her eyes flickered. 'That could work…' And then her gaze was reanimating. 'So you really believe my idea's a goer?'

'I do…'

And even if he didn't, he would still be saying it, because she believed in it, wanted it—not even for herself but to honour Dad's memory, to bring his Lisbon dream to life—and if she wanted it, then so did he—not for Dad but for her—to make her happy, to honour her.

The balance sheet didn't matter. He'd only

chafed at the cost with Dad to provoke him, to cause him grief, because that was the way things were with them. But Dad wasn't here now. Now it was just the two of them and a broken building that needed all the TLC they could give it. Bottom line, whatever it cost, Thacker Hotels could afford it.

For pity's sake, Thacker Hotels could take a hit like this a thousand times over and not feel a thing! And if that meant he was somehow chanting Dad's mantra—fix the building just because—then it was all down to Quinn, because she was filling his well with that glow in her eyes, igniting something bright and kinetic inside him. And he wanted her to see it in him, feel it flowing through him, because she was the one who had put it there.

He took gentle hold of her shoulders. 'I believe in you, Quinn, believe you can create a hotel like no other.'

Her eyes flared. 'Steady on.' But she was smiling with obvious pleasure, blushing, blinding him.

He felt his own face breaking apart, a ripple of pure happiness taking him over. 'I think clients will be banging the door down by the time you've finished. Bespoke boutique! Quinn Radley exclusive design! All in the heart of Lisbon!'

'Whatever you're on, can I have some, please?'

Biting her lip again, drawing his eyes there, making his blood rise, his pulse hammer.

He turned her to face the view, leaning his arms on the rail to stop himself from wrapping them around her. 'It's just this place...' *And you.* 'I mean, look at it...'

Orange roofs...pastel buildings... Castelo São Jorge on the opposite hill, knee-deep in green trees and, to the south, like a blue hem, the mighty Tagus.

'My, but you've got it bad, haven't you?' She was eyeing him softly. 'Like your dad.' And then she was turning to face him, her expression serious. 'So, you're absolutely sure about avant-garde?'

That doubt again. There was only one way to chase it away.

He contrived a solemn nod. 'Absolutely. I'm completely, one hundred percent *for* avant-garde. I just have one question...'

'Okay.' Her eyes narrowed. 'Hit me.'

He paused for effect, clamping down hard on the chuckle he could feel vibrating, then contorted his features into the same look of puzzlement that used to crack Pete up. 'What exactly is it again?'

'Whoa...' Will was holding his arms out, clowning a tightrope walk across the undulating mosaic waves. 'Trippy or what?'

She felt a fresh smile tugging, warmth filling her chest. 'I did warn you!'

He flashed a boyish smile, making her heart skip and tumble, then he was off again, teetering on his way, drawing amused looks from everyone around him.

So funny! So gorgeous!

And so onboard with the exclusivity angle for the hotel. Onboard with jacaranda purple and tram-yellow and Tagus-blue. Giving her licence to do her creative thing, licence to talk about Anthony—not that she had much as yet since, for some reason, it still felt a bit sticky—and being the best company imaginable. Oh, and what about the way he'd taken her arm up there at the viewpoint? That warm, firm grip of his hand then standing so close that she could smell the soapy clean scent of his tee shirt…

'You were right…' He was coming up now, cargos hanging low on his hips, hair blowing in the slight breeze. 'Rossio Square is insane!' He grinned. 'Literally the most fun you can have with your clothes on!'

Her stomach dipped. Way to send her thoughts barrelling in precisely the opposite direction, to a 'clothes-off' scenario! Imagining what those shoulders would look like naked, that chest, that torso. Abs, navel, snail trail…

Oh, God!

And now she could feel a flush spreading upwards from her chest, warming her gills. Could he see it? Was he feeling it too? This crackle on the line, this tingling static.

Maybe.

Maybe that was why he was turning, casting his eyes over the square again—to give them a breathing space, to let the air clear.

'I guess you're already considering mosaics for the bathrooms?'

Safe ground.

She felt her pulse steadying. 'Yes. It's an obvious way to reflect the city.'

He turned back, his eyes twinkling. 'Get me—grasping the obvious! Maybe I'm catching on to this creative vision thing at last.'

'Could be!'

He smiled, then smiled again, hesitantly. 'So, I actually have an idea…'

And again, way to melt her heart. Trying so hard, being so sweet with it.

'Go on…'

'Okay…' Another smile. 'You know that funicular we went on?'

The rattle and clang. Warm air rippling through the carriage. Warm little jolts of his biceps against her shoulder, scorching jolts of his thigh against hers, jolts that sometimes lasted for more than a whole second. But there was something else too, tickling her behind her ribs, sparking mischief. She simply couldn't resist.

'Ahh… You mean Ascensor da Glória… Opened 1885. Electrified in 1912. Two-hundred and sixty-five metres long, ascending forty-four metres, which is, *interestingly*, an eighteen per-cent gradient.'

His lips set, though his eyes were smiling. 'Are you mocking my guidebook again?'

'No, I'm being nice.' She touched her chest, fighting a jag of laughter. 'Showing my appre-ciation. Without your guidebook, where would I be, not knowing all that?'

'Hmm.' His eyebrows lifted. 'You can go off people, you know.'

Borrowing her line, making her arms ache with wanting to fling themselves around his neck. But she couldn't do that again. *Too con-fusing!* She could use one of his own lines back at him though, seeing as he'd started it…

'But not off me, surely…' She hugged herself, preening for effect. 'Because I'm nice.'

He laughed. 'You're a menace, that's what!'

'But cute with it, right?'

Something moved behind his gaze and her heart tripped.

Oh, no!

She hadn't meant to flirt. It had just happened. Because of this sweet charge in the air between them, stealing her focus, his too, from the look of it, which was not good—not good at all! If she didn't sweep this moment clean, and quickly, it was going to get messy.

She licked her lips. 'So, getting back to your idea…' She smiled into his eyes, pushing hard. 'I want to hear it.'

His gaze held her for a loaded beat then it cleared. 'Right. Well, the carriage was covered in graffiti, if you remember, and the walls up the slope too. I don't see much in the tagging, but I think some of the graffiti is cool, and it's everywhere so, you know, it's part of the Lisbon experience.'

Of course it was. There was street art everywhere here.

She felt a smile coming. 'You're right…'

He gave a little smiling shrug. 'Just a thought.'

'A really good one. And quite avant-garde!' Making ideas tingle and rise. 'Maybe floating panels of graffiti because we wouldn't want to overwhelm the space, and with a nod to the carriage itself we could incorporate some curved slat detailing to echo the wooden seats—around the bed headboard possibly, or to divide the room—reclaimed wood if we could get it, for its patina… Oh, and some soft metallic touches to invoke the mechanical—grilles or fretwork—

and maybe a feature naked bulb…you know the ones with the fancy orange filaments…?'

'Sounds great!'

'Take a bow then because it's your idea.'

'Er…*no*…' shaking his head at her as if she were mad '…I said "graffiti"! You've just outlined a whole room concept in the space of five seconds. You're the one who should be taking a bow!' And then his gaze was softening. 'You're amazing.'

Admiration in his eyes and something else too. Something soft… Magnetic… Blue layers shifting, swirling, as if he was imagining…*thinking*… that she…he…they… Her stomach pulsed. Such a tantalising thought, but she couldn't let it be more than that. She was supposed to be helping him, *working* with him, for pity's sake!

Besides, she wasn't a prospect, a safe bet. She was a false flame, a dead end, someone men liked for a while then discarded because she didn't have what it took. And Sadie could tell her she was better than those men till she was blue in the face, but they couldn't all be wrong, could they? Fact was, she was twenty-nine and still single, not by choice.

Not. Like. Will.

Her heart thumped. Because he was a player, wasn't he? Anthony had said so, used to complain about it… She felt her insides tightening. Was that what this was all about—this warm intensity in his eyes a prelude to some well-practised move? Was he measuring his chances, wondering if she would be up for a little weekend fling? Her heart thumped again, harder. But no! That didn't add up, didn't tally. Will was warm, attentive, kind. He was funny. Sweet. She wasn't getting 'player' vibes. Then again, what did she know about vibes? Reading people was Sadie's strength. Sadie, who'd got the measure of Liam right away, while she'd still been tripping the light fantastic, high as a kite on the scent of his roses—

'Hey, are you okay?' Raking his hair back, half smiling, half frowning. 'Don't tell me you get so few compliments that you're actually stunned to silence when you get one.'

'No, I mean…' *Come on, Quinn!* 'Sorry. Thank you. It was nice of you.'

'I wasn't being *nice*.' And then a smile touched his lips, a smile that didn't look remotely like a player kind of smile. 'I was being truthful.'

She felt the air softening, her limbs loosening. Of course he was. Truth in his eyes…warmth, kindness. How could she have let herself think he had casual designs on her? Maybe in some other orbit he was that guy, but not in hers.

'Listen…' He was stepping back a little, pushing his hands into his pockets. 'I don't know what you had in mind for now, but I could actually do with making a few calls before close of business, so maybe I'll shoot back to the hotel for a bit.'

Because he wanted some space? Or was he trying to give her some because he'd detected her minor freakout and thought she needed it? Or maybe he really did have calls to make. *Whatever!* A timeout probably couldn't hurt, although, ironically, suddenly the last thing she wanted was to be apart from him.

'I didn't have anything lined up, but I could do with a bit of sketching time, so if you don't mind me shooting back with you…'

His eyes crinkled. 'Not at all, although, fair warning, when I said "shoot" I really meant "limp".'

She felt a smile rising, all the good feelings rising with it. 'Are you trying to tell me I've driven you too hard today?'

He see-sawed his head and then he split a grin. 'Yep!'

Impossible, irresistible Will…

She felt a smile breaking loose, filling her cheeks. 'I'll bear that in mind for tomorrow then, when I'm planning the itinerary.'

CHAPTER FIFTEEN

HE LEANED BACK in his chair. Praça do Comércio was pretty impressive by night. Buildings all lit up, and that statue too—José I and his trusty horse, Gentil. He felt a smile prodding. Quinn had liked the horse's name but had only just managed not to roll her eyes when he'd told her that the sculptor's name was Machado de Castro.

Fun times! Good food! And still half a bottle of wine to go…

He picked up his glass. Calling that timeout earlier had been the right move. An hour for business, then an hour in the hotel gym followed by a long cold shower had given him time to reset his dial, remind himself that Quinn was a work colleague. Because somehow he kept forgetting. Too high on whatever magic she was sprinkling.

Back there in Rossio Square he'd felt the joy inside cresting, pulsing out of him in waves bigger than those trippy mosaic ones: the joy of feeling good like he used to; the joy of watching her jump on his graffiti idea and spin it into gold; the joy of simply being with her, feeling every single one of his wires connecting. And maybe he had let it show too much, been too intense, like with Louise all those years ago. Maybe that was why Quinn's gaze had gone from warm to wary…

He sipped, swallowed. But things were better now. Even keel. Oh, he couldn't stop himself feeling light as air around her, couldn't stop himself wanting her, but he could keep it inside better—he *must*—because she was who she was, and they had serious work to do.

'Hey…' She was back, sitting down. 'Sorry I was so long. Why are there never enough facilities for we girls?'

Now here was an open goal…

He set his glass down, contriving a pained expression. 'I don't know. We girls do suffer, don't we?'

Her gaze solidified. 'Oh, ha-ha-ha.'

He felt a chuckle coming loose. 'Sorry! Couldn't resist.' He reached for the bottle. 'How about a top-up?'

'Oh, go on then—just the full glass, mind.' And then she was laughing quietly, tucking a stray curl behind her ear. 'I don't know where I heard that, but I can never resist saying it.'

So funny—so lovely!

A thought which was probably dancing a jig all over his stupid face.

Sensible conversation, Will...

'It's a good one.' He refilled her glass then his own, then parked the bottle. 'So, all in all, a good day, inspiration-wise?'

'Definitely!' She scrunched her face up. 'My head's buzzing.'

'I get that feeling too, when I'm about to secure a new hotel site, when it all starts coming together.'

'So, you like the hotel business?'

Surprise in her eyes, in her voice. Perhaps his big, bad attitude to Dad's project had skewed her perception.

'I do but, to be fair, probably not in the way you're thinking. Dad built the business so I signed up, but hotels per se don't excite me. It's the mechanics of business I love, the push and pull, expansion, strategizing and so on...'

'So it could be widgets and you'd be just as happy?'

'Maybe...who knows?'

She grimaced, making him laugh.

'I take it liking business for itself is an alien concept for you.'

'I suppose.'

'So, that begs the question: did you always want to be an interior designer?'

'No...' She picked up her glass, exuding mischief. 'I was aiming for astronaut, but I'm scared of heights so, you know...'

He felt his cheeks creasing. 'Ah, now I get your reluctance to ride the Santa Justa Lift.'

Her eyes flashed. 'You got me!'

'Seriously, though, was it a calling? I mean, I know you studied design, but was it always interiors you liked?'

'Yeah. I like homey stuff, making things nice.' She took a little drink from her glass then set it down. 'My mum was an architect so maybe I inherited something from her—not her patience though! Seven years is a long time to study...' She let out a little sigh. 'Doesn't seem fair that after all that effort she only got to practice for a few years.'

His heart dipped. Because her mum had died in childbirth, hadn't she? Not remotely where he'd meant this conversation to go.

'I'm sorry, Quinn.'

'It's okay.' She gave a little shrug. 'I've had twenty-nine years to get used to it. I don't miss her or anything because you can't miss something you've never had...' Her gaze drifted for a moment then came back, softening. 'Harder for you, I think...'

He felt his blood draining. What was she doing, blindsiding him with Mum like this?! He didn't want to talk about his mother—didn't, ever, with anyone—but if he clammed up it would rock their boat, put a dent in things, and he wanted that even less.

He swallowed to buy a moment. 'It was hard, yes.'

'And now?'

His heart clenched. 'Now it's just awkward, stilted and excruciating.'

'So, you haven't been able to…'

'What? Get over her waltzing off into the sunset with Gabe the hedge fund jerk when I was fifteen?' Because that was what her eyes were asking. 'Strangely enough, no!'

She pressed her lips together slowly. Signalling that the floor was his?

Well, she could take it back because he didn't want it! His heart pulsed. Then again, if he didn't take it, where would that leave them, except on opposite sides of an awkward silence?

He drew in a breath. 'Look, don't get me wrong. I get that she and Dad weren't in a good place before Pete died. I get that Gabe seemed like a better bet than Dad, but after that the only song I can seem to hear playing is the one about how she abandoned me.'

'Which is completely understandable.' She was leaning forward, her eyes welling with kindness, making his own prickle. 'You were fifteen. You'd been through so much already…'

Blue lights flashing… Uniforms at the door… His legs failing… Dad's grey face… Mum curling like a leaf, disappearing inside herself…

He swallowed. 'It didn't seem fair.' He could feel the familiar ache spreading, the familiar hot, thick spot swelling in his throat. 'Not when I tried so hard to take care of her after Pete died. I did everything I could to make her happy, to bring her back to herself, but I failed. And then she left, and I *know* I need to put it behind me, but I can't. She wrecked everything and now I can't look at her the same, can't feel any love…'

Quinn's hand slid over his. 'And that hurts you all over again, doesn't it? Because it's not who you are inside, not the person you *want* to be with her.'

He felt a warm wet swell starting behind his lids. How could she know, articulate so easily what he had never been able to?

He drew in a breath to push it all back, to steady himself. 'Something like that.'

Her hand squeezed his, and then she was taking it back, picking up her glass. 'If you want to move on, you know the only way is to forgive her, don't you?'

Soft gaze. Hopeful light. She made it sound so simple, so doable.

He lifted his own glass, knocking back a mouthful. 'Is that your recommendation?'

Her lips quirked slightly. ‘Well, speaking as a motherless child, with obviously zero experience of mothers, I’d say it’s worth a shot, worth thinking about at least.’

Telling him she didn’t miss what she’d never had, but there was a chink in her gaze saying precisely the opposite—telling him that if she’d been lucky enough to have a mum she would never have let things go stale without a fight.

He felt his heart pinching. Was he an ingrate, too trapped inside his own grudge to see the wider view? Who knew?

He reconnected with her gaze. ‘Maybe I’ll do that then. Think about it, I mean.’

She smiled. ‘You’ve got nothing to lose, everything to gain.’ And then she was setting her glass down, flattening her hands on the table. ‘Right… Didn’t your esteemed guidebook say that taking in a Fado show was a must?’

CHAPTER SIXTEEN

'OH, LOOK—! VINYL!' Will was stopping, taking in the array of tightly packed boxes. 'Do you mind if I have a gander? I love looking at this stuff.'

She felt warmth burling. Every moment something new—something delightful. Gorgeous Lisbon—gorgeous sunshine! And Will, beyond gorgeous in his faded jeans and light orange shirt—seemingly a vinyl addict. Best weekend ever!

She smiled. 'Knock yourself out. I'll go on though. There's a stall up there with some interesting bric-a-brac. Catch me up?'

'Okay.' But then his hand was coming out, staying her. 'No wandering off, mind.'

Her heart dipped. Referencing last night's little misunderstanding in Alfama. To be fair, the protective gleam in his eyes was adorable, a little bit dizzying, but still…

'For the umpteenth time, I did *not* wander off last night.'

'You disappeared.'

'Only into the tile place we were standing right next to!'

'You didn't say you were going in.'

'I thought you saw me. Besides, where else would I have gone?'

His hands went up. 'Who knows? It was dark. There were crowds. My senses were dulled by the Fado singing and you do have a talent for vanishing into thin air.'

Setting his lips but his eyes were crinkling, twinkling blue.

Impossible not to smile, not to capitulate.

She pressed her hands to her chest. 'Okay, Scout's Honour! I promise not to leave the market.'

He grinned. 'Okay, see you in a bit.' And then he was turning, getting stuck in, hunting for jazz, no doubt, which he apparently loved, Miles Davis especially.

She let her gaze linger on his back for a few tantalising seconds then set off.

Feira da Ladra Market—flea market, or perhaps 'thieves' market, Will's guidebook had tendered both. *Whatever!* Strolling round was the perfect lazy Saturday morning activity, a bit of a rest after yesterday and, concerns about her wandering off aside, Will seemed happy—*relaxed*—which was such a weight off after the Judy conversation last night.

She stopped by a rail of vintage dresses, half

looking. She wouldn't have gone anywhere near Topic Judy if she hadn't had two glasses of wine and a golden opportunity. Still, even with licence to talk about Anthony, for some reason actually doing it still felt tricky. Too tricky to risk touching on anything Anthony had put in his letter anyway. But in his letter, Anthony had described Judy's leaving as a 'painful time' and, given that he had never talked much about Judy, and given that she wanted to know Will to his bones, know how he felt about things, she couldn't stop herself from giving him a nudge…

She felt her lungs tightening. And then it had all come out—pain that was more like devastation, trotting out the facts in his man's bitter voice, but the facts didn't make sense to the boy who was still so obviously bleeding inside. And not to her either. After everything they'd been through as a family, couldn't Judy have at least stayed in London until Will finished school? To be around for him, to be a fricking mother! If he couldn't find any love inside for Judy now, then no wonder.

She swiped at the dresses and walked on. But two sides to every story and all that. Forgiveness would be a start if Will could manage it. Not easy. But if he didn't, he would be dragging this stuff around for ever, miserable on some level, just as his father had been, and that was no way to live and, especially, it was no way to die!

She came to the bric-a-brac stall and stopped. There were piles of everything, including a somewhat cool porthole mirror. She leaned over to inspect it. Maybe things wouldn't work out for Will with Judy, but at least he had said he would think about trying to reach out…

'You like, *senhora*?'

It took a second to locate the small, beady-eyed old woman who was smiling at her from across the mountain of lamps and pictures and vases.

'Yes, I do.' She smiled back. 'Can I pick it up?'

'Sim, senhora...' The woman's hands lifted. 'Yes, of course.'

Antique gold…deep frame…filling suddenly with Will's smiling face.

'I'm impressed, Quinn—you're right where you said you be!'

She looked into his eyes in the mirror. 'Of course I am! I did promise. Also, you weren't very long so, you know, not enough time to escape your clutches.'

'Clutches!' His face in the mirror chuckled then disappeared as he came round to stand beside her. 'You make me sound like the Dark Lord.'

'I didn't say evil clutches.'

'Good…' His gaze pinned her for a cloudy beat. 'Because I'm only trying to look after you.'

Way to melt her heart and all of her bones.

'I know. And I appreciate it.' She offered up a smile. 'You're very noble...' Not that she could let herself linger on that confusing thought. 'So, did you buy anything?'

He flashed empty palms. 'No. I flirted with buying something from the Fado section but then I remembered that I don't like super cheery music.'

She felt her insides vibrating. Last night's Fado show was lovely, but after four consecutive slow, impassioned ballads, which to their untrained ears had sounded more or less the same, they'd slipped out to explore the Alfama streets.

'It was all quite heartfelt, wasn't it?'

He grinned. 'Just a bit.' And then his eyes flicked to the mirror. 'So, are we buying that, or what?'

'Not today.' She set it down, smiled an apology at the woman, then propelled him on before the woman could start a sales pitch. 'It's given me an idea or two though, so all good. I'll come back when I know what I'm looking for.'

'Fair play.' And then he was looking over. 'So, what's on the agenda now?'

Aside from crushing on him every single second?

She shook herself. 'If your feet are willing and able, I wouldn't mind seeing the pink street...'

His gaze narrowed. 'I remember seeing that…' And then the guidebook was coming out, absorbing his attention. 'Oh, yes… Rua Nova do Carvalho, former red-light district and crime centre, now über-trendy nightspot. Bars, cafés… Located Cais da Sodré.' His eyes snapped up, full of teasing light. 'Super, a mere ten thousand steps away!'

She felt warmth bursting inside, happiness. He was so good-natured. Such perfect company.

She aimed a smile into his eyes. 'Yes, but then after that, I was thinking we could jump in a tuk-tuk, spend the rest of the day cruising.'

'Yes!' His fist shot up, punching the air. 'I've been waiting for *ever* for you to suggest that!'

Quinn was eyeing him over her glass, patently trying to hold in a smile. 'Are you *dancing*?'

He checked in with his body, felt a chuckle coming. 'I might be…' Because how could he not when the music was this catchy, and the sun was this warm, and the Tagus was yards away, glinting blue? When he was with the kindest, loveliest girl he had ever known. He grooved his shoulders at her for fun. 'What's wrong with a little chair dancing?'

'Nothing…' A smile broke across her face. 'I suppose I just…'

'What?'

She looked shy suddenly. 'I guess I just don't see you as the dancing type.'

'Thanks. No offence taken.'

'Will—' admonishing him with her eyes '—I didn't mean it as a—'

'Black mark on my character?' He took a sip of his beer, letting his smile out slowly. 'Chill. I'm just teasing.'

She gave him the side-eye. 'Not nice!' But then her expression was warming again, brightening with interest. 'So you *do* dance?'

He felt a little sagging sensation inside. 'Well, no, not routinely, so I see your point, but I've had my moments on the dance floor—admittedly, mostly drunken ones when I was a student—but I've been told that I don't totally suck in the rhythm department. What about you? Are you the dancing type?'

'Am I…?' She leaned forward, fixing him with a merry deadpan stare. 'Will, I like dancing so much I dance with my vacuum cleaner.'

In which case…

His heart pulsed. Did he dare? Would the people around them laugh? He felt a smile coming. Maybe he was crazy, finally losing it, but right now he couldn't care less.

He set his glass down and got to his feet. 'Come on then. Show me.'

Her face stretched. 'You're joking, right?'

'Do I look like I'm joking?'

She let out a giggle. 'Sadly, no.'

'So, let's dance.' He held his hand out. 'Unless I'm to be bested by a Hoover.'

'Oh, God!' Rolling her eyes at him, but in the next breath she was parking her glass and getting up, letting him lead her onto the promenade that separated the tables from the river, and then she was standing, staring at him, laughing. 'You're mad, you know that?'

'Yep...'

And if this was madness, then happy days, because it felt great—great to be moving his hips to the beat, letting himself go, seeing amusement shining in her eyes. And now she was moving too, extending her arms with graceful hands, swaying her sublime body this way and that, laughing into his eyes.

So lovely!

Hair up today, loose tendrils grazing her neck. Green vest with a white one underneath, showing those kissable collarbones and that delicious dusky hollow between her breasts. Turning now, rotating her hips, hips he wanted to feel moving under his hands, hands that wanted to slide over that neat gyrating rear, that rear smoothly encased in blue jeans, jeans cropped mid-calf above her white trainers—simple...elegant. Beautiful.

And off-limits!

He spun away. What was he doing, letting his eyes off the leash? Thoughts, desires. So much for cold showers and keeping it in! Why wasn't his body getting the memo? This was Quinn! They had a job to do together, one they both had to get through to get their respective dues.

Gah! But that was the whole problem right there, wasn't it? That this *was* Quinn! Not the cuckoo, not Dad's pet, but something else now, something wonderful. Every blink, every breath of her a blast. Just being with her…talking to her… God, she'd even got him talking about Mum last night, which he never did, with anyone. Listening so well, giving him something to think about, lifting some weight off his chest just by listening, releasing him, so that now he was walking—*dancing*—on air. Oh, and maybe letting his eyes roam wasn't right, but it was only looking, not touching. Only dancing, a bit of fun…

He danced himself back around and started in surprise. There were other people up and dancing with them, going for it! And then Quinn was coming in close, swaying, beaming.

'See what you started.'

He felt his head shaking, words rising. 'Not me. You!'

She pulled a confused face then moved back, laughing, reaching up into the air with her hands.

All very well looking confused but it was true. He hadn't started this. She had. Because he would never have got up with anyone else. It wouldn't even have crossed his mind to, because he wasn't the dancing type, especially not in broad daylight with only a small beer inside him! Only with Quinn, because—spinning again, weaving her hands through the air, circling her shoulders—he felt weightless around her, on fire, light and bright as a flame. And now she was turning, flashing a smile into his eyes, and he could feel his heart soaring, leaping and flying, flowing right out…

Right… Out…

Oh, hell!

It couldn't be, could it? This feeling… Was he somehow falling in love with Quinn Radley?

'Hey…' She was moving in again. 'Where's your groove gone, mister?'

If only she knew!

And then, mercifully, the catchy track was ending, giving him an out.

'Song's finished.' He shrugged, finding a smile. 'I'm afraid one dance is all I've got.'

Her cheeks dimpled. 'Well, I'm glad I got to see it, then.' And then she was giving his shoulder a little nudge, propelling him back to their table through a ripple of applause from the other tables.

He smiled round to acknowledge the crowd. Did he seem normal to them? Or could they see that he was a man reeling? His heart pulsed. Could Quinn?

'By the way, you're definitely not an embarrassment on the dance floor.' Twinkling up at him as he seated her, making his heart flip but also soothing it somehow, settling it back down.

He took his own seat. 'I hope that's not compared to your Hoover.'

'Oh, no! You're way better than that.' Her eyes flashed a tease. 'You're at least as good as my floor mop.'

'Nice!'

'That's the objective!'

Back to banter. Back to easy flow. Maybe he could just tick along like this. His heart clenched. No choice really. It was way too soon to declare himself, or to even know if these feelings were love feelings or crush feelings. His heart clenched again, tighter. And what about the elephant in the room? He didn't feel any animosity for Quinn now, couldn't imagine feeling it ever again, but that gremlin had swooped in once before, hadn't it, ruining everything. Old sores. Like the one with Mum, hurting on and on. Quinn had said if he didn't forgive his mum he would never heal, so it followed that if he didn't somehow come clean to Quinn about her role in his misery, then it could only come back to bite him…

'We should get back…' Quinn was spearing the last olive, popping it into her mouth. 'Miguel will be wondering where we are.'

Miguel. Their smiley tuk-tuk driver, full of mischief and fascinating factoids.

'You're right. We've been a while…' He signalled for the bill then remembered something. 'Hey, Quinn…'

'What?' Twinkling gold-brown eyes.

He felt a warm spot pulsing in his heart, a smile unfurling. 'Thanks for the dance.'

'Here we are! Miradouro de Santa Luzia!' Miguel pulled the little vehicle in sharply then shuffled round in his seat to face them. 'The best place in Lisbon to see the sunset.' His gaze darted to Will then came back, glinting with mischief. 'Very romantic!'

For heaven's sake! He was at it again. Loaded looks, twinkling eyes. Why? Because she and Will had been leaning into each other a lot? Only so they could hear themselves over the road noise! Or was it because Will had handed her out of the vehicle at Belém Tower with an exaggerated gentlemanly flourish? That was just clowning, Will trying to make her laugh. As for the dancing, Miguel couldn't have seen that unless he'd left the tuk-tuk and walked along the promenade and, in any case, it wasn't close dancing, nothing he could read into. She felt a flush stirring. Unless he was reading its lingering effects, the tingles she couldn't stop feeling because of the way Will had been gazing at her, moving his body in sync with hers. A crazy, hazy, über sexy moment! But it was gone now. A bit of fun, that was all.

She aimed a smile into Miguel's eyes. 'You are a very bad man! We've told you already, we're just friends, colleagues…'

'Yes, yes, yes…' He waved a dismissive hand. 'But still, it's romantic. You must go. Enjoy a *ginja* shot, watch the sunset. I can wait…'

Will leaned forward. 'But you already waited an hour in Belém.'

'It's okay.' Miguel shrugged, oozing charm like honey. 'You can give me a very big tip!' He flashed white teeth. 'A very big tip always helps.'

Will laughed. 'Okay, done! A very big tip it is!' And then he was looking over, his expression slightly baleful but twinkling. 'Shall we go check out this sunset, then?'

'Why not…?' Since Miguel wasn't giving them a choice anyway.

A few respectful yards from the vehicle Will started chuckling. 'Miguel's something else, isn't he?' He smiled over. 'Worth every single euro, though!'

She felt her heart softening. 'Yes…'

Not just Miguel, though. Will was something else too. Every kind of wonderful. Liam would have been walking through this little park chuntering, not chuckling, feeling manipulated by the Brazilian, not seeing what Will had clearly seen: that Miguel was poor, needed all the tips he could get.

If only Miguel knew that he needn't have given Will that wily little push because Will was generous, would have tipped him handsomely anyway. All the time, rewarding good service, being subtle about it. Like at that tapas place. Slipping two blue notes under his glass as they got up to leave—more than the bill itself had come to. And yes, he could afford to be generous, but not everyone with money was, unless they were angling for something for themselves. Liam. Roses. Case in point!

She pushed the thought away, focusing ahead. They were stepping onto a wide pillared terrace now, lush with clambering vines, teeming with tourists. A woman was selling *ginja* sour cherry liqueur shots from a stall at the side and a busker was perched on the parapet playing soulful guitar, but it was the view opening up through the crowds that stopped her breath. Lisbon and the Tagus, the sun behind painting everything gold.

'Wow!' She looked up at Will. 'Miguel was right. This is incredible!'

'It is.' He smiled, making her breath stop again, but then suddenly his gaze was going past her, lengthening. 'Hang on. There's a better spot…' His eyes snapped back, full of mischief. 'Ready to run?'

Her heart pulsed. 'What?'

But his hand was already grabbing hers, tugging her through the crowds, until they were at the very end of the terrace where the parapet butted up to a high sheltering wall. A quiet spot, almost secluded.

He released her, panting a bit. 'Sorry for the mad dash, but it's a prime spot.' He motioned to the parapet. 'You can sit and chill with the view while I go back for some *ginja*.'

She felt her heart squeezing. All this for her!

She smiled. 'It's perfect, but please don't worry about the *ginja*…'

'What? And disappoint Miguel. No way! You know he's probably got a commission thing going on with the *ginja* woman, right?' And then his eyes were crinkling. 'Besides, don't you want to taste it? It's like a thing here. We should give it a go…'

So adorable. And so very sexy with his hair blowing in the breeze, sun gold turning his blue eyes green. Her stomach pulsed. All the things she shouldn't be noticing!

She shook herself, smiled. 'Okay, you've convinced me. We can be Ginja Ninjas.'

His chin dipped. 'Seriously?' And then he was chuckling, shaking his head. 'So lame!'

'This is lovely.' Quinn was sipping, tasting her own lips. 'Sweet!' And then she was looking up, a little glow in her gaze. 'Almost as sweet as you with Miguel.'

'Sweet?' He forced his eyes not to revisit the lips she'd just tasted. 'I've never been called sweet before.'

'Well, you are.' She wrinkled her nose. 'My ex would have whinged about being leveraged into giving a big tip.'

He felt his stomach tightening. The thought of Quinn with anyone else, especially a tightwad, was a total gear-grind.

'Sounds like a right jerk.'

'Oh, he was.'

At least she wasn't holding onto any candles!

He took a sip from his cup. 'Miguel's shirt is patched in three places, and his trainers are coming apart. He isn't well-off. Also, he's been great—pleasant, knowledgeable. He deserves a good tip.'

'Which you'd have given him anyway, without

him having to ask.' Her gaze softened. 'You're so tuned in, Will. Sensitive, just like your dad said...'

His heart caught. 'What...?'

Because Dad had never said anything like that to him, given him any indication he had ever noticed anything on the fricking inside of him at all! Just the bad stuff. Faults and failings. Blackjack, whisky, women. He would never shut up about those.

She gave a little shrug. 'He just said it...'

But then she was blinking, her cheeks colouring as though she was wishing she hadn't mentioned it.

His fault. Because he was suddenly tight as a drum. Spine, shoulders, jaw. Reacting in spite of what he felt for her, in spite of himself, in spite of asking her not to skirt around the subject of Dad.

What he had meant was that she shouldn't skirt around her affection for Dad, around the hotel and the plans they'd made. But *this*...this was a curveball, a real stinger. Why had Dad never dipped below the waterline with him, taken *him* aside to say stuff like this? Why tell Quinn? And now, what? Was she waiting for him to pick up the baton, chat on merrily as if his gut wasn't wringing itself tight? Was she expecting him to light up with interest, ask her what else his own father had divulged?

His heart pulsed. *Not fair, Will!* Strain, showing on her face, in her eyes, because she was caught in the middle again—caught there because he had asked her to be open, asked her not to tiptoe around him and Dad, caught there because she was doing exactly that!

He needed to level out, say something.

He set his cup down to buy a moment then met her gaze. 'I'm sorry for freezing like that. I…' He could feel his heart pinching, his throat drying. 'I'm just surprised. I didn't know Dad thought that about me…'

The planes of her face softened. 'Oh, Will, he did…' And then her eyes were welling, glistening into his. 'He just wasn't very good at expressing it.'

'Except to you, apparently!'

Her eyes closed and regret crashed in. Why had he said it like that, in a whiplash tone? He felt his insides twisting. How to walk this impossible line? Half of his heart lost to her, the other half bitter. And now the two halves were tearing him apart because he'd been cruel when none of this was her fault.

'I'm sorry, Quinn…' He seized her shoulders so that she would feel his regret, all the desperation inside. 'Please… Please look at me… I didn't mean it…'

'You did…' She screwed her face up tightly,

swallowing, and then her eyes opened, blinking into his. 'But I don't blame you, Will...'

He felt his throat constricting. Why not? Did she get him, understand somehow, in spite of everything? And if so, could she see how much it meant, see how the warmth she was giving out was turning him inside out, making him want to...?

'Oh, Quinn...'

And then somehow her face was in his hands and he was moving in, brushing her lips with his, taking her mouth. Soft... Warm... Cherry sweet... His pulse spiked...*responsive!* Rising towards him now, sliding her arms around his neck, kissing him back, tasting him back. He could feel his blood heating, beating hard, pent-up desire dragging at him, taking him over. He wanted more...to give more, so she would feel his love, feel it from the very heart of him—deeper. Warmer. He teased her lips apart with his tongue, felt the brief incendiary touch of hers, but then, all of a sudden, she was pulling away, pushing at his chest.

'Stop, Will. Please.'

He jerked his hands away, heart pounding. 'What?'

'We mustn't.' Closing her eyes, swallowing, shaking her head as if it was a battle to get the words out. 'I want to, so much. But I can't...'

He felt a protest rising, collapsing. Telling him what he already knew, what he'd told himself over and over again. They had a job to do, one that would go easier if they kept their relationship on the straight and narrow.

'You're right. I'm sorry.' He inhaled to steady himself. 'We're working together. Mixing it up is probably a bad idea.'

'Yes...'

He felt a spike of adrenaline. That 'yes' lacked conviction, as if it was only half an answer. And there was something flickering through her gaze that felt like a hammer blow coming. He could feel himself tensing, bracing in anticipation.

'It isn't only that, though...' She pressed her lips together tightly. 'It's that I don't want to lose you.'

He felt his heart pausing, the tightness inside relenting. 'But you wouldn't...' Because wasn't getting together the exact opposite of losing each other?

'No, I *would*...' And then her gaze was turning inwards, full of anguish and latent fury. 'I'm single for a reason, Will! I'm no good at relationships. No one ever stays with me.' Her hand caught his, squeezing hard. 'And I couldn't bear it if that happened with you.' And then, maybe because the confusion he was feeling was showing on his face, her voice tipped over into impatience. 'Don't you see? I've got too much to lose... You're the last and only link to a huge part of my life!'

The words seemed to hang in the air, echoing, reverberating inside his skull. So this was the punchline? The lethal blow. That he was nothing but a link to Dad?

He felt his blood draining, a hot swell rising behind his eyes. Falling for her, getting tangled up in the thought of her... All this time thinking about not crossing over work lines, but somehow stowing a secret hope in some secret recess of his heart that once the work was done...

Idiot, Will!

Hung up on 'some day' when what she was offering was never—because of Dad! Because of this precious link—to what, exactly? Because Dad was gone, and he was...

His stomach turned. What was he? Other than sick. Heart. Belly. Soul. He couldn't think, speak, vent, couldn't even let it show, because Quinn had a right to her feelings, same as he did, even if they were incomprehensible. And he couldn't freeze on her because of the hotel. Nothing to do then but suck it up, stay behind the line she was drawing.

He swallowed hard. 'Fair enough.' He squeezed her hand gently to seem onside, then put it away from him, forcing out a smile. 'No hard feelings, right?'

For a long second her eyes searched his, as if she wanted more, expected more, but what more could he say—*give*—when simply holding himself upright was taking every ounce of strength he had? And then, finally, she blinked.

'Of course not.' She smiled a smile that looked like his own felt, and then she turned back to the view. 'Look, the sun's gone down.'

His heart flinched.

And didn't that just sum it up!

CHAPTER SEVENTEEN

SADIE INHALED AUDIBLY. 'What happened after that?'

She felt her heart crimping. What had happened was trudging back to the tuk-tuk feeling depleted, faking jollity all the way back to the hotel for Miguel's sake, then bursting into tears in her room because all she'd been trying to do was share a fragment of Anthony with Will, to make him happy. But it had backfired, made him hostile instead—which she totally got because Anthony should have told Will all that stuff himself. Then somehow her understanding had backfired as well, making Will's gaze go all soft and intense...

And then the kiss had happened, and it had felt so right, like heaven, until confusion took hold, shook her up. And even though she was the one who'd pulled away, and even though Will had smiled and said 'No hard feelings', and even though he'd brought her all the way home from the airport, joking about being nice to the last because of their pact—which surely demonstrated that everything was all right between them—she wasn't feeling all right at all, which was why she was on the phone to Sadie at midnight, keeping the older woman from her shelter duties.

She swallowed down a sip of tea. 'We went back to the hotel, muddled through dinner. And this morning we had to be at the airport for ten so… Probably a good thing.' Her heart pinched. 'He insisted on bringing me home from the airport though, which was nice.'

'*Very*, given that he lives on the opposite side of London.' Little pause. 'So, now you're in turmoil…'

Her heart pinched again. 'What do you think? I just don't know if I did the right thing, putting the brakes on. My head says yes, but I don't know…' Because for a moment, after she'd explained herself to him, Will had looked broken, and it was messing her up, messing with her heart. Seven hours back—seven hours churning away over it, seven hours reliving that kiss: the tenderness of it, the warm, perfect fit of his mouth, the hot, dragging ache of desire that was still dragging. She swallowed hard. 'I just can't seem to think straight.'

'Well, let's start with those brakes.' There was a small pause while Sadie sipped her own tea. 'Why *did* you put them on?'

'Because it would only end in disaster.'

'Why?'

Her chest went tight. 'You know why!'

Sadie sighed. 'I'm taking you through a process, Quinn. Please answer...'

She closed her eyes. 'It would end in disaster because all my relationships do.' She felt a flick of weariness. 'You know that, Sadie. I'm not a safe bet. And this is Will! I'm supposed to be helping him find himself. If things went bad between us then, for a start, that plan's a bust. I'd be failing Anthony, denying him his dying wish. And I'd be losing everything that's been dear to me for the past decade. I'd be emotionally homeless.'

'So, the head has spoken. What's the heart saying?'

'I don't know, hence the phone call.'

'Okay, well, perhaps we need to slide some doors.'

She felt a smile coming. Sadie was invoking her favourite movie.

'Door one: you keep the brakes locked on and you and Will stay friends. Maybe you become best friends! Hanging out. Brunch on Sundays! Sometimes you go double dating. The Thacker connection is strong with you...'

Invoking Yoda now!

'But then the day comes, which it will, because

I've seen his picture in Tatler and he's gorgeous, not to mention seriously loaded, which shouldn't factor but, you know...' little breath '...the day comes when Will gets married. He asks you to be his best woman. Nine months later, he asks you to be godmother to his firstborn. Your Thacker connection is sealed, eternally assured.' Sadie's voice filled with a knowing twinkle. 'How does that sound?'

'Unappealing.' She parked her mug on the bedside table. 'Can we do the other door?'

'We don't have to. You're already rattling the handle.'

True.

She plucked at the duvet. 'Maybe I am, but should I be? I need advice, Sadie. I don't know what to do, or how to feel. Please, tell me what you think.'

'Oh, Lordy...' Sadie drew in a weighty breath. 'Are you sure you want to hear?'

'Yes.' Because Sadie was older, wiser, the closest thing she had to a mother. Plus, Sadie was generally right about everything.

'Okay, well, for a start, I think you're head over heels in love with him.'

Her heart paused. *Impossible!* Because Will was practically a stranger. Yes, she liked him. A lot. Cared about him a lot. And yes, he was under her skin, but only because he was a bit damaged, and that kind of thing always tugged at her heartstrings.

As for those other tugs and tingles she was always feeling around him—the ones that happened when his eyes crinkled or his nice shoulders shifted—par for the course, surely, because, as Sadie said, Will was gorgeous. And yes, his kiss had put the hex on her, got her craving and pining, which symptoms maybe did bear some resemblance to a love type of yearning, but equally, it could just be a physical thing—infatuation! Just a stupid crush playing her for a fool, trying to turn her against the door one scenario, which was clearly the most sensible and enduring one.

She adjusted her grip on the phone. 'I think you're wrong.'

'Well, let's pretend I'm not. Let's pretend that you and Will love each other, so we can deal with your biggest fear: that if it doesn't work out, you lose your connection to the Thacker family.'

'All right…'

'Question: what would you actually be losing? I mean, to be blunt, Anthony's gone. You'll always have your memories, *that* connection, but you never met Judy, and you never had much to do with Will in the past, so if things were to end, then, aside from losing a straggle of random outliers, what is there, really, to cling to, except an idea? And I know how important the idea of family is to you, I know you were devoted to Anthony, and I get why you've taken his dying wishes to heart, but what I think—straight up—is that you're letting your loyalties get in the way, and pointlessly.

'Anthony did a good thing by you, Quinn, but by his own admission he made plenty of mistakes in his life. It seems crazy to me that you'd deny yourself a chance at love with Will for his sake, especially when Will clearly has feelings for you too.'

'Oh, God, Sadie…'

Way to mess her up even more, dangling possibilities from Will's side—possibilities that, thinking about it… She felt her heart giving.

The way he'd turned round at the airport and come back, guidebook in hand. The way he'd pulled her over to the railing at Miradouro de São Pedro to reassure her he was all for avant-garde—not just for it but coming up with ideas of his own! Clowning all the time to make her laugh. Confiding in her about Judy. Oh, and dancing by the Tagus! Looking out for her all the time, taking care of her. Keeping tabs. Always capitulating…apologising…trying. Bringing her home from the airport for the sake of their stupid pact, bent on showing her his nicest side. She felt her throat constricting, tears welling. As if he even had any other side!

'And as for this business of helping him find his so-called light, you seem to think it must be something he plucks out of himself, that it shouldn't have anything to do with you, but what if it does?'

Her heart stumbled. 'What?'

'I'm saying, what if Anthony meant *you* to be Will's light?'

Her heart stopped dead. 'Don't be daft—Anthony wasn't matchmaking! He didn't think like that. He was categorically the most unromantic man I've ever known.'

'Well, tying you both into a prolonged hotel renovation sounds like a pretty foxy move to me.'

'But he…'

Sadie wasn't right. Couldn't be. Could she? What did it matter anyway? Anthony was gone, so there was no asking him. No making sense of anything.

'I can hear your cogs whirring, Quinn.' Sadie sighed. 'Maybe the best advice I can actually give you is to stop thinking so hard.'

'After just giving me a whole lot more to think about!'

'It's only conjecture. What isn't is that Will saw you to your door, which shows he's trying to right the ship.' She paused. 'You can come back from this. The project's a long one. You've got time to work things out, get to know each other better. Who knows, maybe you did the right thing, calling a halt this time.'

'What do you mean, *this time*?'

'Just that I think there'll be a next time…' And then there was an extended pause, a sense of distraction. 'Listen, love, I've got to go. Fred's signalling through the door. Looks like trouble in the dorm.'

'Okay, go!'

But Sadie was already gone.

She parked her phone and sank back into the pillows. How not to think about Will and everything that went with him? How not to miss him… want him? Still, as Sadie said, they had time, and maybe that was exactly what she needed. Time to straighten out her head, and find out what was really going on in her heart.

CHAPTER EIGHTEEN

MARION'S HEAD BOBBED round the door. 'I'm off now.' Her eyes made a quick assessing sweep of his face. 'There's a plate in the fridge for you.'

As if he could eat anything while his brain was burning like this. But if he didn't show her some enthusiasm she would only worry. Bizarre that the housekeeper seemed to care more about him than his own mother did.

He smiled into her eyes. 'Thanks, I'll get it later.'

'Make sure you do.' Her lips flattened. 'You look tired.'

'I am…' Tired, wrung out, confused, sad. Could she see it? No matter. He wasn't up for talking about it. He smiled again. 'Have a good evening, Marion.'

'You too, Will.'

Footsteps echoing, fading. Door banging. Silence.

He got up to refill his glass then slumped back down on the sofa. Could it really be that all he was to Quinn was a link in a chain she didn't want to break? If so, wouldn't he have felt it, seen it for what it was? Or was his lens so twisted by love that he'd put a rosy spin on that light in her eyes, seeing it as warmer, fonder, deeper than it really was?

He drank, felt the whisky burning. No. Yesterday, it had definitely felt like it, but now he wasn't so sure. Maybe his lens was rose-tinted, but the way she'd leapt up to hug him when he found her in that café was real. Pure joy. All weekend long, that same feeling: connection, affection. Back and forth. He wasn't imagining it. And he wasn't imagining the way she'd kissed him back either, all warm, sliding her arms around his neck. Pulling away but in the same breath saying she wanted to—*'so much'*—but couldn't because all her relationships went bad, that she couldn't bear it if it happened with him, couldn't bear to lose him. Then the sucker punch. That stupid, precious, incomprehensible link!

His heart paused. Then again, was it really so incomprehensible?

He sat forward, swirling his drink. She was an orphan. All out of links, all out of family—except for his. And maybe his family didn't amount to much now, but still, if it was all she had… He felt his heartbeat picking up. Would she not cling to it like a raft, even at a subconscious level, perhaps find the fear of losing it surfacing involuntarily at the wrong moment, say, in the middle of a kiss, find it asserting itself as suddenly as his own scars were prone to doing, rupturing in an instant, putting whiplash words into his mouth at precisely the wrong fricking time! It was absolutely possible. So slow on the uptake, Will! The writing was blazoned on the wall. Quinn volunteered at a homeless shelter, for pity's sake, giving her time and attention to those enduring the thing she most feared—*dreaded*—being without: loved ones. Ties. Roots. Place!

He felt his heart twisting. All things he could give her, wanted to give her from the depths of his soul. He set his glass down. But he'd jumped the gun because of his own messed-up history, because of his own messed-up head, because she seemed to get him, understand him, and he was so desperate to be understood by her. Accepted. *Loved.* But desperation was a poor hand, one he wasn't playing again.

He got up and went to the window. Twilight now...bats flitting. He felt his pulse settling, the mist clearing. Lucky for him he'd taken her home, leaning on the pact they'd made, because it had seemed like a good way to bounce them back from that kiss, show her that from his point of view they were good. And yes, maybe there was a part of him that had been hoping she might open up the conversation, which she hadn't, but they'd parted on smiling terms, which meant he had a head start now. He would call her tomorrow, fix up a lunch, show her she wasn't lost to him, that he wasn't about to break any links.

And maybe he was crazy for letting that hopeful voice inside start whispering *some day* again, but he didn't want to switch it off, didn't want to kill off his hope yet. Not when time was on his side, when he could use it to show her that he was steadfast, dependable. That he could be a sound business partner and, most of all, a good friend. Maybe then she'd come to see him as a win-win prospect!

CHAPTER NINETEEN

THE CAB PULLED up and Will smiled, mischief glinting in his eyes. 'Here we are!'

She looked out and started. 'Lisbon!' She felt her jaw trying to fall against a rising smile. 'I had no idea there was a restaurant called Lisbon in London!'

'There isn't.' Will handed the driver a twenty with instructions to keep the change and then his eyes came back, twinkling. 'I paid a guy to re-paint the sign. It's really called The Lucky Star Takeaway.'

Her smile won out. How she'd missed this—*him!*—even though it had only been four days since she'd last seen him.

He sprang the door. 'Come on. Sadly, I'm on the clock.'

On the clock but making time for her all the same, calling her the day after they'd got back. Business lunch, Thursday! What it felt like though, was that he was trying to smooth things out, get them past that kiss. But smooth was good, exactly what she needed. Or maybe it was just the sweet, sweet sight of him she needed.

Whatever! Right now, she was floating on air.

Inside, the host led them through a sea of white damask and glittering crystal to a table by the window. A prime spot—of course. *For her.* Her heart pulsed. It was all for her. This beautiful restaurant, this table overlooking the Thames…

She swallowed hard and turned to meet his gaze. 'This is amazing, Will. Thank you. Such a view!'

His eyes crinkled. 'I'm glad you approve. I figure if we're talking business, we might as well do it in style, right?'

In style, in a blur. It felt like the same thing. A fantastic dream. And then somehow their plates were being cleared and their glasses were being replenished, and the rest was falling away so it was only Will again, smiling over, drop-dead gorgeous in his business suit.

'I'm curious…' He inclined his head. 'What got you volunteering at the homeless shelter?'

Drop-dead gorgeous and working so hard. All through lunch talking earnestly about the project, and now he was switching tracks to keep them running along smoothly. The problem was that his efforts seemed to be having the opposite effect, drawing deep, velvety warmth up through her, fresh longings. She couldn't seem to stop her eyes from drifting to his mouth, and to that patch of golden skin at the base of his throat where his collar was open. And she couldn't stop remembering the way his lips had felt, what that brief, sweet scorch of his tongue had done to her body, her core—

'Quinn…?'

Eyes. Face. So dear. So beautiful. So utterly—OMG! Her heart pulsed. It was true! Everything Sadie said. She could feel it surging inside, rampaging through her veins. How could Sadie have seen it and she not? She was absolutely mad for him, past saving. Head over heels in love.

Her heart thumped. But she couldn't say it, go anywhere near it. Not after shutting him down like that in Lisbon, not when loving him didn't guarantee a happy ending—not when she needed to process and couldn't, because he was taking up all of her bandwidth. Nothing for it but to dig deep and push through, as if climbing over the table to kiss his face off was the last thing on her mind.

She forced herself to swallow. 'Sorry. I was just thinking about my friend Sadie…' Not a lie, and a neat segue! 'I got involved through her…' She felt a ripple of calming warmth at the thought of the older woman. 'She's my friend now, but back in the day she was one of my design tutors. She set us a brief to design an interior space for a homeless shelter which was compliant, functional, nurturing. I liked that she specified "nurturing". It felt generous of spirit.'

He smiled a tingle-inducing smile. 'I like it too.'

'Anyway…' She blinked to reset. 'Turned out Sadie was a volunteer. I don't know why but the idea spoke to me so I asked if I could go along.' She felt a flick of incredulity. 'That was ten years ago. Sadie's full-time now, and I'm still there…'

He let out a short, astonished breath. 'Wow! And what do you actually do?'

'Street patrol, mostly. Checking in with the rough sleepers, seeing that they're okay.'

'Okay being a relative term?'

'Sadly, yes. We try to get them to come in, especially the women and girls, but a lot of them don't like the shelter. Some of our service users have mental health problems, addictions. They can be disruptive, aggressive sometimes.'

His eyes flared. 'So, it's dangerous?'

'Potentially, but the permanent staff are trained to deal with it. Volunteers are trained too but generally we don't encounter problems—verbal abuse sometimes, but most of the rough sleepers don't mind us. Some of them like to talk.' She felt an ache in her chest. 'They get lonely, feel invisible.'

'You are officially blowing my mind.'

Admiration in his gaze, tugging at her strings, making her blush.

She reached for her glass to deflect. 'Do you do anything outside work?'

His expression fell. 'Nothing useful or remotely noble.' He touched a finger to the base of his glass as if he was toying with a thought, and then his eyes flicked up. 'Until quite recently, I was a regular at Aspinalls.'

Her heart pulsed. And now, what? He wasn't a regular any more? *What to say?* She sipped to buy a second. Maybe he just wanted to talk about it.

She set her glass down. 'Anthony did mention the casino.'

His lips flattened. 'Oh, I'm sure he did! The old goat didn't exactly approve.'

She felt a stir of recognition, took care to make her tone gentle. 'Was that the attraction?'

His ocean-blue gaze stilled. 'Very perceptive!' And then he was picking up his glass, tilting it this way and that. 'Lest you think I'm bitter and twisted, it wasn't all spite.'

She felt her heart twisting. So hard to see him hurting like this, ridiculing himself, because that was what was going on behind the bravado—pain, hurt, bitterness. If only she could tell him how much Anthony had loved him, how deeply he regretted his mistakes, but last time it had backfired, and she couldn't risk it again. Not here. Not now. Better going with the tide.

'So you *like* gambling?'

'Not exactly…' He took a hefty sip and then, unexpectedly, he broke into a smile. 'I liked counting cards.'

Her ribs went tight. 'But isn't that—'

'No, it isn't illegal.' He shrugged. 'It's just arithmetic. Exercise for the brain.'

'There are other ways.'

'So I've discovered.' His gaze fell for a beat then lifted, attached to a wry smile. 'I mean, what's bigger and more exciting than gambling on a bespoke boutique hotel in the heart of Lisbon, right?'

'You're getting a gambling thrill out of it?'

'No!' His features drew in. 'I was joking, Quinn.' And then he was shaking his head, his gaze softening. 'But if the thought of me gambling bothers you then I won't do it ever again.' His chin dipped a little. 'Is that what you'd like: for me to promise?'

Depths in his eyes…depths within depths.

She felt her stomach tingling. So Sadie was right about this too. He did have feelings for her, strong enough to change his ways, do for her what he wouldn't do for his father.

Her heart pulsed. So, there were feelings running both ways then, but she couldn't act on hers, not after Lisbon, and, for the same reason, he was unlikely to either—aside from giving her lunch at the best table in the house and a heartfelt promise to quit gambling, neither of which she could think about right now when he was looking at her like this, waiting for her to reply.

She nodded, pressing her gaze into his, loading it with all the love inside. 'I would, Will. Very much.'

'Okay, I promise—Scout's Honour—no more gambling.' He smiled. 'From now on, I'll apply my brain only to work and to our hotel!'

And then he was talking about dessert, something about a 'deconstructed' Portuguese custard tart, but it was fading in and out because all she could hear playing over and over were the two words that she'd never heard him say in the same breath before.

Our. Hotel.

CHAPTER TWENTY

HE DROPPED HIS holdall and pulled out his phone. It had pinged as he was riding up in the lift and it could only be Quinn, replying to the text he'd sent from the taxi.

He tapped the screen, felt a smile breaking loose. Quinn indeed!

Sorry Budapest negotiations are dragging. *sad face emoji* To cheer you up, master suite WILL be finished tonight if it kills me and it is going to be FAB-U-LOUS! So sad…aka furious…that you're in meetings all evening and can't video call. Even sadder that you're not here to share the moment because it feels like a milestone and Filipe is no fun at all. I'm in his bad books because the bathroom fittings I ordered from Paris have been delayed again which means the plumbers can't get on and now this is 'holding up the whole project'!!! Anyway, hope your meetings go well tonight and that Team Thacker prevails. I'll send pictures of the finished suite! See you in London next week. Q x

He slipped his phone back and went to the window, staring out over Rossio Square. If only she knew he wasn't in Budapest! He felt his smile fading, his stomach tightening. Coming here to surprise her like this was tantamount to pinning his heart on his sleeve, wasn't it? Putting himself on the podium, finally. Then again, hadn't he been on this trajectory ever since that 'Lisbon' lunch three months ago? A supposed business lunch that had ended up with him promising to give up gambling for her.

Transparent, much!

As was going out on street patrol with her and Sadie that night in London, love, and admiration, leaking out of him the whole time. As for taking her along the coast to Cascais last month for her birthday, obvious surely, unless her other friends also took her for champagne lunches on yachts!

He felt warmth unfurling. Her face that day—all smiles on deck. Hair bound up with a colourful scarf, blowing in the breeze, her long brown legs killing him in white shorts, her eyes aglow with fifty shades of mischief.

'You're spoiling me, Will! Not that I don't totally deserve it because I'm the one who's here, putting up with Filipe!'

Later, they'd found a park to walk through,

trees and cacti cohabiting in a magical dappled woodland, and after that, back in the charming little town, they'd happened upon a gallery, and that abstract in oils of the 25 de Abril Bridge that she just 'had to have' for the master suite because it was 'perfect'!

His heart pulsed. Perfect, like every moment was with her. Catch-ups and debriefs in London, but also Sunday brunch as friends. Portobello Market, galleries and jazz clubs—because education cut both ways! Always fun, always easy. And maybe that was because they didn't feed the demon by talking about Dad, or maybe it was because Quinn had a warm, wonderful way with her but, whatever it was, he was feeling good on it. Drinking less, taking care of himself. He was even looking into the issues around homelessness—not that he'd mentioned it to Quinn yet—talking to the board about Thacker Hotels doing something significant in that regard.

And here, the hotel was coming on apace, which was down to Quinn and the team, but he was keeping his finger on the pulse too, extending himself, even discovering a bit of chutzpah he never knew he had! He felt a smile coming. That was what Quinn had called it anyway, when he'd persuaded Michelin-starred chef Xavier Rankine to leave the Aurelia in Paris to take control of their restaurant. Opening was six months away still, but Rankine was going to put them on the map. As was Quinn's luxurious avant-garde décor…

He felt his heart softening. Giving her all, spending days at a time here to get things done. Did she really think he wouldn't have crawled through broken glass to be here to celebrate her completing their flagship master suite? Wild horses couldn't have kept him away. Because she was everything now, and he wanted her to know it, feel it, and maybe he was misjudging, misreading her signs, but at the same time it didn't seem possible because every time they were together he could feel the air crackling two ways.

He crossed the room to the mini-fridge. The bottle of fizz was there, just as he'd asked. And two flutes. Damask napkins to wrap them in.

Champagne, then dinner at her favourite place. After that, who knew? He flicked a glance at his watch. But first, a run to calm his nerves. Then it would be time to give his favourite interior designer the surprise of her life!

The plastic sheeting round the door rustled frenetically then disgorged Filipe.

'Hey, Quinn!' His eyes darted to the painting she was unwrapping—the striking abstract that she and Will had found in Cascais. 'It's seven. Everyone else has left. Are you coming?'

In other words skedaddle, which was *not* happening!

She smiled to placate him. 'No, not yet.' She scanned the rich blue wall—blue for the Tagus—fixing on the blank space where the painting was to go. 'I'm on a roll, Filipe, so close to finishing…' And it wasn't as if she had anything better to do since the one person—*the only person*—she would have walked off the job for wasn't here. She turned back to him. 'You don't have to wait. I've got my keys. I know the alarm codes.'

He peeled off his safety helmet. 'You shouldn't be here alone.'

She forced her eyes not to roll. He meant well but he was such a stickler!

'I know, but I'll be fine, honestly. I mean, the hallways are clear. I'm not going to trip over any ladders, fall through any—'

Her heart clutched then fluttered, spraying tingles. Oh, the way Will had caught her that day, crushing her against him—so quick, so strong. Nothing to how he was now though! Honed from every sublime angle, skewing her senses every time they were together. It was getting harder and harder not to say something, not to throw herself at him, especially when he was close, when she could feel sparks crackling between them, hear the rhythm of his breathing actually changing around her. When he was so damn attentive and indulgent! Champagne lunch on that yacht for her birthday, then discovering Cascais: that beautiful, lush little park, that amazing gallery. And coming on street patrol with her in London, winning Sadie right over, and herself even more. Signs all the time. Tingles all the time.

But nothing was moving forward. He didn't talk about Anthony, or Pete, so she didn't feel that she could either, even though she wanted to. Stuck for weeks, revolving in the same old doors, and it wasn't enough, God help her. She wanted more: to know more, give more, feel more, emotionally…physically. She wanted to love him, drown in his heat, feel his body on her, inside her, everywhere. God, just the thought of it was misting her up, stealing her…

Brakes! Now!

She blinked, reconnecting with Filipe's frowning gaze. 'Look, if I finish tonight then I can get back to London a day sooner. I've got clients backing up that I really need to deal with…' Was he caving? Maybe a tease would clinch it. She angled her head, smiling into his eyes. 'Plus side: you get to *not* have me around tomorrow, messing up your schedules.'

His frown softened. 'Fine! But please text me

when you leave so I don't spend the night worrying about you.'

She felt her heart softening. He could be such a grump, but he was kind to the marrow.

'I promise.'

'Okay.' He nodded a smile then turned, fighting his way back through the plastic. 'Goodnight, Quinn.'

''Night, Filipe.'

She listened to his boots crunching down the hall then pulled out her phone. Nothing more from Will. Her heart pinched. Stuck in Budapest when he should have been here, sharing this!

She tapped, setting her Miles Davis playlist going—Will's favourite, growing on her too. She parked her phone, surveying the room to 'Moon Dreams', felt her mood lifting. This was nice work at least!

Finishing touches!

She felt a tingle, a smile coming. Maybe she could send Will a little video of the finished rooms, do her grandiose TV presenter impression to make him laugh. He'd like that.

She picked up her scissors, bending to the package again, but then her heart lurched. Footsteps—coming along the hallway. A heavy, purposeful stride. Filipe? *Of course.* She felt her breath flowing out on a wave of relief. He must have forgotten something.

She straightened. 'Filipe? Is that you?'

'No, it's me!'

Her heart stopped, then vaulted. 'Will!'

And then the plastic was rustling, parting, and he was appearing. He set a bag down on the floor, casual as anything, and then he was looking up, smiling. 'Hello!'

She couldn't move, couldn't breathe. He looked so gorgeous—tanned, scrubbed…better than heaven. And she was in her oldest paint-spattered jeans and vest, wearing *eau de fresh paint* if she was lucky!

His eyes flicked to the scissors in her hand. 'Are you going to put those down or are we re-enacting *The Shining*?'

She felt the dam breaking, joy bursting. 'What the hell, Will?' And then, before she could think a single thought, the scissors were falling and she was launching herself at him, flinging her arms around his neck. 'You came!'

'Did you really think I wouldn't?' He was laughing into her ear, hugging her back, all warm and tight. 'Like you said, milestone moment…'

She closed her eyes, breathing him in. It was so good to see him. But what was she supposed to do with all this leaping joy, all this love inside? How did she get from here to where she wanted to be?

She swallowed hard. 'So it was all a ruse—late-night meetings?'

'Yep! That was last. We got it all signed off this morning.'

'So you thought you'd have a little fun?' She felt her lips curving. 'I hate you!'

He chuckled softly, his breath warming her ear. 'Yeah, I'm kind of getting that.'

But he wasn't pulling away, wasn't disengaging, not even slightly. If anything, he was enfolding her more, pulling her closer. She could feel his muscled torso through his shirt, her body responding, her nipples hardening. Could he feel her—feel her heart beating, the bubble of happiness bursting, spreading inside her? Because something was changing, altering the air, the mood, the temperature. Definitely the temperature!

She felt a sudden, crushing desire to cry. Because the point was past now, wasn't it, for stepping back as if there was nothing between them? It was long gone. Without a word. No more pretending. No more holding back. Too late now to step back into the spin of those doors. This was a sliding door moment, and she was sliding, for better or for worse. She could feel her hand moving to the back of his neck, her fingertips touching the hair they'd been itching to touch for months.

'Oh, Quinn…'

His voice was low, urgent, wringing tears out of her, putting a crack in her own.

'Don't ask me to stop, Will, please…' Because

touching him was all she wanted to do. Skin. Hair—glorious hair…soft, thick, slipping between her fingers just so.

'I'm not asking you to stop…' He was breathing into her hair, nuzzling, his lips grazing her temple. 'But I need to know…' And then he was pulling back, taking her face into his hands, stroking her cheekbones with his thumbs. 'Are you sure?' His eyes were reaching in, drinking her in, as if he couldn't get enough. 'Because I can't go down this road with you if you're not sure…' His expression tightened. 'It would kill me, Quinn.'

She felt her heart giving, her whole body tightening and tingling to his touch as if she were an instrument he was playing. 'I'm sure, Will. Please…' She closed her hand around a fistful of hair, pulling him towards her a little. He resisted for a beat, the ghost of a smile on his face, and then he was coming for her, his lips taking hers, bold, confident. Such a perfect mouth! Such a perfect fit…so warm. She felt the scorching tease of his tongue and parted her lips, letting him in. She could feel her heart exploding, or maybe it was her pulse. She was liquid, melting, wet between her legs already. Could he feel it through her jeans because his hand was there now, as if he knew she needed just that.

'Oh, Will…' It was involuntary, from the depths

of her. She felt her hands going for his shirt buttons, tearing at them until she was touching smooth, hot skin.

'Quinn…' His lips were on her neck now, his hands roaming, torturing her nipples, sliding down, cupping her butt, drawing her in hard against him. 'Have you any idea how much I want you?'

She felt her breath coming in short bursts, a smile breaking. 'I can feel it.' Rigid along his considerable length, a length she couldn't wait to unwrap. She went for his zip, just as he gripped the hem of her vest.

'You first.' His eyes were hazy, hooded. She did the honours, button, zip, then raised her arms so he could peel off her vest.

For a long moment his eyes gazed at her and then he leaned in, kissing her mouth again. 'You blind me, Quinn.' And then she was being lifted, swung up into his arms. 'Do we have such a thing as a bed?'

She was trembling inside, weak with longing, lost in the warmth of him, the strength of him.

'Yes, we have a bed. Super king-size, dressed to the nines!'

Quinn put her glass to her lips, eyes twinkling. 'I didn't anticipate christening the master suite quite like this…'

He felt his heart swelling. Quinn, naked. Almost too lovely to look at. Was this real or was he dreaming? Had he really just been inside her, losing himself in her sighs, feeling her body rising, exploding with him, blowing all his fuses at once? Not how he'd expected that hug to turn out, but he was so glad about it, so freaking happy!

He bent to kiss her shoulder. 'Me neither.'

'Are you sure…?' She raised her eyebrows. 'I mean, you did come prepared!'

He felt a flash of warmth around the gills. 'Keeping a condom in my wallet is an old habit…'

Wait! Was she laughing at him? He felt a beat of ease, a smile loosening.

'I've had a few shameless moments in the past, all right—I admit it.' He slid his eyebrows up to tease her back. 'I didn't hear you complaining anyway!'

She laughed. 'Nothing to complain about!' She took a sip from her glass then set it down, smiling. 'You're not just a pretty face is all I'm saying, lover boy.' And then she was snuggling in close, nuzzling his neck. 'God, you must think I'm fickle as hell, tearing your clothes off after saying no last time, but those things I said before stopped making sense to me weeks ago. I've been going crazy since then.'

So he had been right then, about the air crackling both ways. He felt warmth spreading, stowed his glass so he could lie down and draw her into his arms. 'I'll bet I've been going crazy for longer.'

She moved her head back a little, eyes locking on his. 'So now you've got my attention, William Thacker.' A smile touched her lips. 'How long?'

Silver angel...

'Since the night of Dad's sixtieth.'

Her gaze stilled. 'But you didn't even talk to me! You left early.'

His stomach pulsed. Questions in her eyes—questions he should have seen coming if he'd been thinking straight, thinking at all, instead of oversharing.

And then she was shifting, sitting up, her gaze curious. 'Why *did* you leave that night?'

What to say? That he'd hated himself for finding her attractive when she was the one who'd supplanted him in Dad's scant affections?

He raised himself up, angling himself to face her. 'It's complicated.'

'I'm good with complicated.' Kindness in her eyes. 'Please, Will...'

His heart gave. If he didn't try, didn't risk the vortex, what was the point of all this? Making love—*love*—not having sex. Wanting her, weaving dreams around her. If he didn't brave this then it was all for nothing, and he couldn't bear the thought of that. But he couldn't bear the thought of hurting her either, so it was thinking of a way in, a gentle way, a way that would give her a shot at understanding.

He shut his eyes, inhaling to find some clarity, then met her gaze. 'I guess it's all to do with Pete really…' And here it was arriving, right on cue, the burn, the ache. Throat. Eyes. Always the same. He swallowed, blinking back hard. 'He was everything to me, Quinn. Brother. Friend. Protector, in a way.' He felt a smile trying to rise past the pain. 'He was so funny. Brought it out in me too. Man, the way we carried on, laughing till our sides were aching. Over the stupidest things. He had this infectious laugh, you know, that sort of kept yours going…

'He was popular. Good at sport, good at everything. He could have let it go to his head, but he didn't. He was kind. Thoroughly decent.'

'Like you…'

Her gaze softened, but he couldn't let himself get lost in her warmth. He had to get through this, finish somehow.

'It wasn't just me that worshipped Pete.' He felt his ribs tightening. 'Mum did, lit up when he came in the room. As for Dad, God you should have seen him, smiling like a normal fricking parent, slinging his arm around Pete's shoulders…'

Her hand touched his forearm. 'Breathe…'

He inhaled, steadying himself. 'When Pete

died, Mum tuned out. Dad got even more hooked on work. I felt—*was*—invisible. I tried telling myself we were all grieving, tried to help Mum, and I told myself to cut Dad some slack. But we were a sinking ship. And then Mum left, so all I had was Dad, except he didn't make himself all that available.

'I figured it was up to me to push, because I needed a parent, Quinn, needed to feel that *I* mattered. I interested myself in Dad's stuff: the Morgan he was rebuilding; the business. As soon as I was sixteen, I asked him if I could work at Thacker in the holidays. I wanted to ride into work with him, show him I could be useful, that he could be proud of me.

'It took a bit of time, but things got better. We were getting on, doing all right, but then…' He looked into her eyes. Was she seeing it, getting it yet? He didn't want to actually say it—*couldn't*.

And then suddenly it was there in her gaze—recognition. Then tears welling.

'Then I came…' She blinked, throat working. 'I came between you, didn't I?'

He felt his heart seizing. 'You didn't mean to, I know that.'

'That's why…' Her gaze turned inwards. 'Oh, how could I have been so blind? So much is making sense now. You were always backing out of rooms at home. You never spent holidays at the cottage.' Her eyes came back to his, glistening. 'You couldn't bear the sight of me, could you?'

His heart wilted. 'For a long time, no...' This had better prove cathartic in the end because it was causing a lot of pain. He swallowed. 'At Dad's sixtieth, you were dazzling. I wanted to come over. I wanted to dance with you, hold you, and I couldn't bear myself for wanting it, because you had Dad's ear, his time, all the things I didn't, so I left. But it wasn't your fault. Any of it. It was Dad's. I made an effort for him, but he never did the same for me. He never got me, Quinn, never even tried...' He could feel the burn again, the tearing ache, the boy inside howling. 'He never loved me because I wasn't Pete. I wasn't golden, good enough, ever! No matter what I did, no matter how many hours I put in at Thacker.'

'No, Will! No!' She was shaking her head now, throat working. 'You're wrong, so wrong, about your father.'

His heart pulsed. Was she actually defending the old man?

'What do you mean?'

'Anthony *loved* you, Will... So much.'

Wet eyes, reaching in, making it worse somehow, making his blood pound.

'Well, excuse me if that went right past me.'

'He did! He was sorry for everything that went wrong between you.'

His body tightened like a zip. 'Which you would know, of course, because he talked to *you*, didn't he?' He could feel his gorge rising, dredging all the old animosity back, and for some reason, maybe because she seemed to be siding with Dad, he couldn't make himself stow it. 'Dear old Dad, bending your ear, confessing to his favourite saint, instead of—here's an idea—taking the direct route—taking the time and trouble to talk to me. You never thought to tell him that!'

'Stop it, Will!' Her eyes flashed. 'I *get* that you're hurting, I do, but please listen. He made mistakes but he cared about you. It's all in the letter he wrote me—it's why he wanted me on this project with you. He asked me to help you, be your friend…'

His lungs emptied.

No... It couldn't be true. Everything they'd shared had felt spontaneous. *Real!* He felt his teeth clenching, grinding. But it wasn't. Yet again, this wasn't about him. It was about Dad. *Pleasing* Dad! Being his friend *for Dad*. Doing it all *for Dad*. All…

He felt his eyes looking at their tumbled sheets, a hot wave rising inside, rising and rising. From the bottom of his trashed heart he did not want to hurt her, but why should he be the only one hurting when there was so much hurt to go round?

He sprang from the bed. 'And did he ask you to sleep with me as well?'

Her face paled. 'How dare you?' And then her mouth was tightening, her eyes blazing white-hot fury into his. 'Get out, Will!' Rising up onto her knees, as if making herself taller would make her louder, more emphatic. 'Get out! Now!'

His heart caught, but only for a beat, and then the bile was back, hurtling through his veins. 'Oh, don't worry yourself, Quinn.' He snatched up his clothes, heading for the door. 'I'm already gone!'

She felt the words ringing in her ears, stinging, reverberating, her throat thickening, hot tears sliding out, tickling her cheeks.

Will...

How could he have said such a thing, even thought that Anthony, that she...?

She felt a shudder taking hold and sank down, pulling the sheets up around herself.

He couldn't think it, believe it.

No! She drilled her fingertips into her temples. *No, no, no.*

He was only venting, striking out like a wounded animal because she'd spoken up for Anthony, trying to defend him, intercede. Lashing out because of all the pain inside, hurt he'd hidden behind a façade—drinking…gambling…casual encounters which didn't require trust. Hurt he'd kept bottled when he should have let it out to those who should have listened, who should have been strong enough, brave enough, to take it, instead of copping out—Judy, Anthony!

Her throat constricted around a sob. And unwittingly she'd made it so much worse. All those years of coming in, only to find her and Anthony together, finding them laughing maybe. She felt her chest heaving, another sob rising. Oh, she could see it all now through Will's eyes. Her hand on Anthony's arm. Her arm linked through Anthony's when they were walking to the pub. Sitting by him on the sofa, getting him to watch the kind of movies she used to watch with Dad. Popcorn! Trying to make Anthony into Dad, trying to coax him into being what he wasn't, what he'd never been, and all because she'd needed a parent, needed it so badly that she couldn't see what she was doing to Will, dislodging him from the spot he'd fought so hard for. Bad enough trying to fill Pete's shoes without having to battle her as well. No wonder he'd left all the time. No wonder he'd resented her.

No wonder! Her heart clenched. *Stupid, Quinn!*

Blind to the last, to the very end. Even while the red flags were going up—that tightness along his jaw, that cool edge sharpening in his gaze—she'd just kept on talking, hadn't she? Banging Anthony's blasted drum in his face, hellbent on trying to help, but all she'd done was push him over the edge and now he was gone.

She felt fresh tears scalding. Love light in his eyes just hours ago, *making love* to her right here, taking his tender time with her, pouring himself into her until she was helpless, out of her mind with pleasure and love… Rare… Precious… *Real!* Her heart reared up. Not something to let slip through her fingers, not when it had taken her this long to find it. She might have given Will his marching orders but she loved him, heart and soul, and she wasn't letting him go. This wasn't the end!

Phone!

She'd call him, apologise, beg him to come back, and then they'd talk, sort all this out.

She scrambled off the bed and ran into the other room, but before she even got to her phone the pressing silence declared everything she didn't want to know. Dead battery. Killed off by Miles Davis. And of course her charger was at her rental apartment. And Filipe had asked her to text. She felt a flick of panic. What time was it? If Filipe was trying to check in and couldn't get through, he might come back, might be coming up the stairs right now!

She looked down at her naked body and dived for her clothes, dragging them on quickly. The room! She ran back in, straightening and plumping, hauling the massive silk bedspread into place. Filipe had remarked on it just that morning, so she couldn't leave it anything less than pristine. Then it was the bottle and the glasses, napkins, wiping and tidying. Ridiculous to be chambermaiding when what she needed to be doing was hightailing it after Will.

The Metropole. He always stayed there. He was bound to be there.

Please, God, let him be there!

CHAPTER TWENTY-ONE

HE PUSHED THE great door shut and dropped his bag.

Silence.

But of course. Because Marion wasn't expecting him back today and Dad was—

He pulled in a breath. Just as well. He was in no fit state for company. What he wanted was a drink.

In the office he poured a Scotch, knocking it back as he went to the desk. He was so tired. Tired of fighting. Tired of reacting, of revolving inside these same old doors. He sank into his chair, forcing his gaze through the leaded panes to the giant beeches at the outer reaches of the garden.

Oh, Quinn...

She was right to have sent him packing. He'd been cruel, out of order. But only because of this festering sore inside that he needed to lance and drain. The boil of Dad. His heart pinched. And yes, the boil of Pete too. How it hurt, turned him inside out to admit it, but he had to face it. He'd loved Pete to his bones, but after he died he'd resented him too, for shining so brightly, for leaving Mum bereft, Dad, all of them, aching and angry. To have that much hold, so that functioning without it was impossible, wasn't healthy. No one should have that much power!

He rubbed his hands over his face. But power only gripped if you let it and he couldn't, not any more. Fighting with Quinn had shattered more than his heart. It had snapped his strings, floated him free. Oh, he'd been seething, yes, bruised and broken all the way to Rossio Square, but then he'd remembered her stricken face, her eyes wide with shock and disbelief and hurt, and remorse had cracked him open.

He'd turned back, calling her over and over, getting voicemail over and over because she was blocking him, shutting him out. And then, standing outside, surveying the burnt-out shell of himself, he'd realised he would be no good to her anyway, no good to himself, until he'd dealt with the demons inside, forced himself over one last hurdle.

He put his hand to the drawer and pulled it open, taking out the envelope Edward had slid over the desk to him an eternity ago…

Dearest Will,

Already I imagine you curling your lip at my salutation, but whatever you think you are dear to me, dearer than you could ever imagine. My admiration for you knows no bounds.

You are strong, Will. And sensitive. A powerful combination. You succeeded where I failed, conquered your natural reticence and shyness to reach out to me, but I couldn't conquer my demons in turn and be the father you needed, deserved. I go to my grave knowing that I have failed you as utterly as I failed your brother. Yes! Failed him too, beyond redemption. I should have leaned on you, Will, confided in you, but something inside me wouldn't allow it. So now I must write out my guilt, burdening you further, for which I am deeply sorry.

Pete was killed because of me. Because I refused to drive him to rugby practice. Mum was out that day, if you remember. It was raining. Pete came into the office, asking if I could take him. Three miles. Only three miles, but I said no, because I was busy. I told him to take his bike. He was good about it, the way he always was.

'Okay, Dad. It's fine.'

The last words he ever said to me.

Now you have even more reason to hate me, but know that you will never hate me as much as I hate myself.

My message to you, Will, is to live your life free of me, because I am not worthy of your pain. All very well, you must be thinking, when I have tasked you with finishing my Lisbon hotel, but my reason for doing that is not to irk you, but to appeal to your great good spirit and do one thing for me.

Please, take Quinn into your fold. Be a friend to her. She is worthy of your time and your affection. I promised her father to take care of her because he didn't want her to be alone in the world, but now I must leave her, and she will take it hard. Quinn is good at hiding her issues behind her smile, behind her warm, generous nature, but she needs an anchor in her life, and I urge you to be that anchor, Will. I hope that in working together you will become friends. It is my dearest wish that you do.

I love you, Will. Try to remember that.

Dad

Oh, Dad...

He felt his chest heaving with a sob, tears scalding his eyes. Why hadn't he said any of this before, to his face?

Oh, God! And Pete… *Pete!*

That day. Rain slanting down. And Mum was out, yes, visiting a friend in hospital. He'd been in the kitchen, raiding the fridge, when Pete had stepped in, backpack on, hands tightening the straps of his bike helmet.

He'd flashed a grin. *'See you later, squirt!'*

The last words he'd ever heard from Pete's lips.

He drew in a deep breath, wiped his eyes then looked at the photo he kept by the phone. Pete smiling straight towards the lens. His own smile directed at Pete, as it always was.

'See you later...'

And he had expected to see him later, never thought that… And Dad wouldn't have thought it either, that Pete would never come hurtling back through the gates, spraying gravel the way he always did. Dad had been busy. But he was always busy, always working weekends, building the business. And for a seasoned cyclist like Pete, three miles was nothing, even in the rain. How many other dads hadn't driven their kids that day and got lucky, got their kids back safe and sound?

He felt his heart cracking, tearing. Why had Dad kept it to himself? He should have let them in, told them, let them all talk about it. Yes, he would still have felt guilty, of course he would, but maybe a little less so for sharing, a little closer to him and Mum for sharing. Who knew? The only thing for sure was that life was precious—too precious to waste fighting and hiding from the people you loved.

His heart pulsed. And the one he loved most of all, loved with all his heart, was where? In Lisbon? In London? He slipped the letter back and got to his feet. He had to find her somehow. Tell her everything, *share* everything, so he could start living his life—a life he couldn't imagine spending, that he was categorically *not* going to spend, without her.

She swiped her card and slipped through the opening gates. Would he be here? His car was, every sleek black inch of it, but he might well have taken a cab to the airport so that didn't say much. Her heart twisted. If only she'd managed to catch him before he'd checked out of the Metropole but, rushing, she'd dropped the stupid champagne bottle, wetting the bedroom carpet, and she couldn't leave it like that. She'd had to clean it up, crying the whole time because she couldn't call him or the Metropole to leave a message, or even a cab to come pick her up and speed her there to make up for lost time. And then it was too late. But it had seemed that he might come home. So here she was.

She drew in a breath, heart pounding, and set off across the familiar gravel to the familiar blue door—imposing, immaculate. She glanced at the knocker. Ought she to knock, or use her key? She bit her lip, opting for the key, but as she pushed it into the lock the door gave sharply inwards.

'Quinn!'

Will!

Weary-looking. Blotchy, as if he'd been crying.

He let out a short, astonished breath. 'What are you…? How…?' His hands mimed an exit motion. 'I was just coming to look for you.'

'Where?'

As if that was even important, but he was answering anyway.

'Lisbon. London. Wherever you might be…' He shook his head as if he thought that maybe she wasn't real, and then his gaze was clearing, opening into hers. 'But you're here, thank God.' And then his face was crumpling. 'I'm sorry, Quinn, so, so sorry for saying what I said, for being cruel, insulting. Unfair.' His hands lifted in a gesture of hopelessness. 'I didn't mean any of it. Please, tell me you know that.'

She felt her heart constricting. He was taking the blame again. Always taking the blame. Not this time though.

'I do. Of course I do. But it's not your fault, it's mine. All of it. It's why I'm here. To say sorry that I stole Anthony from you.'

'You didn't…' He was shaking his head, frowning. 'Dad was never available to me, not really. He never would have been—'

'Yes, he would…' She could feel her eyes prickling, a lump clogging her throat, but she had to say it, confess all. 'I couldn't see it before, but after our fight I could, so clearly. When I first moved in, I remember that you and your dad did talk, that things were normal, seemed normal between you. But then you went to uni, and I had him to myself…

'I didn't mean to do it, but I latched onto him hard, Will, trying to make him like my dad, because I missed my dad so much, the way we talked, the things we used to do… I missed—still miss—the way Dad was with me, that closeness we had. And Anthony was so good to me—of course he was—but the truth is, he wasn't like Dad, not at all. And I keep imagining how we must have looked to you, walking arm in arm, sitting together watching movies, but it wasn't what it seemed. *I* was always the one linking my arm through his, not the other way round. And *I* always picked the movies we watched, made the popcorn, trying to do movie night, but he'd often pick up a book halfway through, or fall asleep.'

Will twisted his mouth to one side. 'He always was an old curmudgeon.'

Was he actually trying to make her laugh right in the middle of her heartfelt speech? The one she'd rehearsed all through the flight! *No matter.* She was finishing this if it killed her.

She tightened her gaze on his. 'That's my point. What you saw, backed away from, was as much fake as it was real. Your father was difficult, Will. Troubled. He found it hard to show affection. But underneath I always felt he was a good man, and I miss him. But he wasn't my father, he was yours. And I'm sorry for any pain I've caused you.'

'Oh, Quinn.' His eyes were glistening, smiling at the same time. 'Just come here, will you?' And then he was pulling her inside, pushing the door closed, taking her shoulders in his hands. 'None of it matters. Now I've read Dad's letter I know that for sure.'

Her heart pulsed. 'You've only just read it?'

'Yes.' His lips tightened. 'I stuffed it in a drawer the day I got it because I thought it would be full of rubbish, Dad trying to justify the terms of his will.'

Which, from the look in his eyes, it wasn't.

She felt her heart flowing out to him, her hand going to his cheek. 'Do you want to talk about it?'

His gaze softened and then he broke a smile full of heart-stopping warmth. 'I do. I want to talk about everything, but not right now.'

Oh, that light in his eyes, darkening to a haze, giving her all the feels, all the happy tingles, making her lips curve, her eyes want to cry. 'So, what did you have in mind for right now?'

He chuckled and then he was leaning in, lifting her chin with his thumb. 'I have a notion to kiss the woman I love then take her to bed.' His lips brushed hers, sending a tingle thrilling through her body. 'What do you think?'

She closed her eyes. How could a heart feel so much joy and relief, so much love for one person? And he loved her too, and they were going to work everything out. She felt her lips curving, smiling into his mouth, felt him smiling back. 'I think being kissed and bedded by the man I love with all my heart sounds absolutely perfect.'

EPILOGUE

Six months later...

'WOULD THIS BE the moment to remind you that not every idea you have is a good one?' Quinn was looking at him, half smiling, but also perturbed. 'I mean, seriously, you want us to take a tuk-tuk ride when the Hotel Antonio opens in T minus ten seconds?'

He looked at Miguel. 'She's prone to hyperbole. We open in three hours, and we have staff in place.'

Miguel grinned then looked at Quinn. 'Please get in, *senhora*?'

The perfect accomplice!

'Fine!'

She got in.

He slid in beside her and then Miguel was taking off, hurtling the little vehicle down the narrow street.

He held in a smile. If he'd learned anything about Quinn over the past year, it was that she was a grafter. She couldn't bear to take her hands off the wheel, even for a second, but it was all under control.

He looked over, catching her smile, feeling his heart flip and tumble.

Beautiful Quinn. Saving him. Filling his heart with happiness every second of every day. She was a primary colour. Like Pete. And soon, hopefully, she would be *his* primary colour. It was what this little excursion was about, because what better day to ask her than this one? The opening of the Hotel Antonio, named for Dad, of course. Because why wouldn't they have called it after him? For all his faults he'd brought them together, and that called for some heartfelt recognition!

Quinn looked over. 'Where are we going then?'

He glanced at Miguel. 'Nowhere really. Just driving around.'

Her eyes narrowed. 'Why?'

'Because otherwise you'd be running around like a headless chicken, and you need to stop and breathe.'

'In a moving tuk-tuk?'

'Yes.'

'Hmm.'

They were entering the Praça do Comércio now, approaching their destination. He felt his veins tingling. Time for part one!

'Miguel, could you please pass me the bundle?'

Miguel obliged.

'What's that?'

He wanted to laugh. She was like a meerkat on fast forward. 'It's something I've been working on that I want to give you.'

Her eyes lit. 'A gift?'

'Sort of…' He handed it over. 'Open it.'

She lifted the flap, pulling the papers out of the envelope, scanning the pages, and then she was looking up, her eyes filling with tears. 'You're building a village for the homeless?'

He nodded. 'That's the plan.'

Her lips wobbled then stretched. 'Why?'

He felt his own eyes tearing up. 'Because there's a need. And because I can. And because it means a lot to you.'

'Oh, Will.' And then she was launching herself at him, hugging him tightly. 'I love you so much.'

And there went his heart, bursting again. He wrapped his arms around her, burying his lips in her hair. He lived for this, for pleasing her, because she pleased him all the time, blew his mind, all the time.

He breathed her in. 'It's not settled yet. I can't put it into action until we've been running Antonio for three months and the will comes into effect, but the board is on board, so to speak.'

She took his face in her hands and kissed him. 'It'll happen, I know it, because you're driving it, and you're the best.' And then she was smiling into his eyes. 'Totally worth taking time out for. Thank you.'

And then she suddenly seemed to notice that they'd stopped. 'This isn't driving around. We've stopped.' Her eyes narrowed. 'Why have we stopped, Will?'

Miguel was turning in his seat, smiling fit to burst. 'Because we have reached our destination.'

'Arco da Rua Augusta?'

He felt a smile rising. 'Yes.'

Miguel's eyes flicked to his then to Quinn's. 'So, I'll leave you alone for a few moments then…'

Way to give the whole thing away!

'What's going on?' Quinn was eyeing them both suspiciously, the ghost of a half-smile on her lips.

'Nothing…' He patted his pocket covertly, checking for the ring box, then leaned back against the seat, trying to hold his smile in tight. 'Nothing at all.'

* * * * *

If you enjoyed this story,
check out these other great reads
from Ella Hayes

One Night on the French Riviera
Barcelona Fling with a Secret Prince
Their Surprise Safari Reunion
The Single Dad's Christmas Proposal

All available now!